Holiday Wishes

By Jill Shalvis

Heartbreaker Bay Novels

SWEET LITTLE LIES

THE TROUBLE WITH MISTLETOE

ONE SNOWY NIGHT (novella)

ACCIDENTALLY ON PURPOSE

CHASING CHRISTMAS EVE

HOLIDAY WISHES (novella)

Women's Fiction Novels

LOST AND FOUND SISTERS

Lucky Harbor Novels

SIMPLY IRRESISTIBLE • THE SWEETEST THING

HEAD OVER HEELS

LUCKY IN LOVE • AT LAST

FOREVER AND A DAY

IT HAD TO BE YOU • ALWAYS ON MY MIND

ONCE IN A LIFETIME

IT'S IN HIS KISS • HE'S SO FINE

ONE IN A MILLION

Animal Magnetism Novels

ANIMAL MAGNETISM

ANIMAL ATTRACTION

RESCUE MY HEART

RUMOR HAS IT

THEN CAME YOU

Holiday Wishes

A Heartbreaker Bay Christmas Novella

JILL SHALVIS

AVONIMPULSE
An Imprint of HarperCollinsPublishers

Excerpt from *About That Kiss* copyright © 2018 by Jill Shalvis.

Sweet Little Lies bonus scene copyright © 2016 by Jill Shalvis.

HOLIDAY WISHES. Copyright © 2017 by Jill Shalvis. All rights reserved. Printed in the United States of America. No part of this book may be used or reproduced in any manner whatsoever without written permission except in the case of brief quotations embodied in critical articles and reviews. For information, address HarperCollins Publishers, 195 Broadway, New York, NY 10007.

Digital Edition NOVEMBER 2017 ISBN: 978-0-06-246358-6
Print Edition ISBN: 978-0-06-246360-9

Cover art by Nadine Badalaty
Cover photographs: © Lucky Business/Shutterstock (couple); © Sunny Images/Shutterstock (stars); © altafulla/Shutterstock (wood)

Avon Impulse and the Avon Impulse logo are registered trademarks of HarperCollins Publishers in the United States of America.
Avon and HarperCollins are registered trademarks of HarperCollins Publishers in the United States of America and other countries.

FIRST EDITION

17 18 19 20 21 QGM 10 9 8 7 6 5 4 3 2 1

Holiday Wishes

Chapter One

To say Sean felt stressed was a huge understatement. Give him a cliff to scale or a bar brawl to break up. Hell, give him a freight train to try to outrun, *anything* but having to pull off being the best man for his brother Finn's wedding—including but not limited to keeping said brother from losing his collective shit.

It's not like Sean didn't understand. Getting married was a big deal. Okay, so he didn't fully understand, not really, but he wanted to. He really did. And how funny was that? Sean O'Riley, younger brother, hook-up king extraordinaire, was suddenly tired of the game and found himself aching for his own forever after.

"We almost there?" Finn asked him from the backseat of the vehicle Sean was driving.

"Yep."

"And you double checked on our reservations?"

"Yep."

"No, I'm serious, man," Finn said. "Remember when you took me to Vegas and when we got there, every hotel was booked and we had to stay at the Magic-O motel?"

"Man, a guy screws up one time . . ."

"We had a stripper pole in our rooms, Sean."

Sean sighed. "Okay, but to be fair, that was back when I was still in my stupid phase. I promise you that we have reservations—no stripper poles. I even double and triple checked, just like you asked me a hundred and one times. Pru, I hope you realize you're marrying a nag."

Pru, Finn's fiancée, laughed from the shotgun position. "Hey, one of us has to be the nag in this relationship, and it isn't me."

Sean held up a palm and Pru leaned over the console to give him a high-five.

"Just so you know," Sean said to Finn, "I didn't pick this place, your woman did."

"True story," Pru said. "The B&B's closed to the public this entire weekend. Sean booked the whole place for our bachelor/bachelorette party weekend extravaganza."

"I superheroed this thing," Sean said.

Finn snorted and let loose of a small smile because they both knew that for most of Sean's childhood, that's what he'd aspired to be, a superhero—sans tights though. Tights had never been Sean's thing, especially after suffering through them for two seasons in high school football before he'd mercifully cracked his clavicle.

After that, he'd turned to fighting, and not the good kind either. Finn, physically older by seven years, mentally older by about a hundred, had single-handedly saved Sean from just about every situation he'd ever landed himself in. Thanks to Finn, there'd been a lot fewer situations than there should've been and it hadn't been for lack of trying.

Fact was, everyone knew Sean had taken the slowest possible route on his way to growing up, complete with plenty of detours, but he'd hit his stride now. Or at least he hoped so because Finn was counting on him in a big way over the next week and Sean had let him down enough for a lifetime. He wouldn't let him down now.

Sean pulled into the B&B's parking lot and turned to face the crowd he'd driven from San Francisco to Napa. And he did mean crowd. They'd had to rent a fourteen-seat passenger van to fit everyone, and he was the weekend's designated driver.

Oh, how times had changed. "Ready?" he asked.

Finn nodded. Pru was bouncing up and down in her seat with excitement. Willa, her BFF, was doing the same. Keane, Willa's boyfriend, opened the door for everyone to tumble out.

It was two weeks before Christmas and the rolling hills of Napa Valley were lined with grape vines for as far as the eye could see, not that they could actually see them right now. It was late, pitch dark, and rain had been pouring down steadily all day, which didn't detract from the beauty of the Victorian B&B in front of them. It did, however, detract from Sean's eagerness to go out in the rain to get to it though.

Not Pru and Willa. The two raced through the downpour laughing and holding hands with Elle, Colbie, Kylie, and Tina—the rest of Pru's posse—moving more cautiously in deference to the preservation of their heels. Sean, Finn, and Finn's posse—Archer, Keane, Spence, and Joe—followed.

They all tumbled in the front door of the B&B and stopped short in awe of the place decorated with what had to be miles of garland and lights, along with a huge Christmas tree done up in all the bells and whistles. This place could've passed for Santa's own house.

Collectively the group "oohed" and "ahhhed" before turning expectedly to Sean.

This was because he was actually in charge of the weekend's activities that would lead up to the final countdown to the wedding happening next week at a winery about twenty minutes up the road. This was what a best man did apparently, take care of stuff. *All* the stuff. And that Finn had asked Sean to be his best man in the first place over any of the close friends with them this weekend had the pride overcoming his anxiety of screwing it all up.

But the anxiety was making a real strong bid right at the moment. He shook off some of the raindrops and started to head over to the greeting desk and twelve people began to follow. He stopped and was nearly plowed over by the parade. "Wait here," he instructed, pausing until his very excited group nodded in unison.

Jesus. He shouldn't have poured them that champagne to pre-game before they'd left O'Riley's, the pub he and Finn owned and operated in San Francisco. And that he was the voice of reason right now was truly the irony of the century. "Stay," he said firmly and then made his way past the towering Christmas tree lit to within an inch of its life, past the raging fire in the fireplace with candles lining the mantel . . . to the small, quaint check-in desk that had a plate with some amazing looking cookies and a sign that said: YES, THESE ARE FOR YOU— WELCOME!

"Yum," Pru said and took one for each hand.

She hadn't "stayed." And neither had Finn. They both flanked Sean, munching on the cookies.

A woman sat at the check-in desk with a laptop, her fingers a blur, the tip of her Santa hat quivering as she typed away. She looked up and smiled as she took in the group. That is until her gaze landed on Sean and she froze.

He'd already done the same because holy shit—

"Greetings," she said, recovering first and so quickly that no one else seemed to notice as she stood and smiled warmly everyone *but* Sean. "Welcome to the Hartford B&B. My name's Charlotte Hartford and I'm the innkeeper here. How can I help you?"

Good question. And Sean had the answer on the

tip of his tongue, which was currently stuck to the roof of his mouth because he hadn't been prepared for this sweet and sassy redheaded blast from his past.

It'd been what, nearly a decade? He didn't know exactly because his brain wasn't functioning at full capacity, much less capable of simple math at the moment. The last time he'd seen Lotti, they'd been sixteen-year-old kids and at a high school football game. It'd been back in those dark, dark times after he and Finn had lost their parents and Sean had been at his most wild. Still, he'd somehow managed to sweet-talk the kindest, most gentle girl in school out of her virginity, losing his own in the process.

Finn nudged Sean, prompting him to clear his throat and speak. "We're here to check in. We're the Finn O'Riley party." He smiled. "It's really great to see you, Lotti. How're things?"

She cocked her head to the side and looked out the window. "Well the storm's certainly been challenging. I heard the roads were bad, so wasn't sure you'd all even be able to get here. I'm glad you made it. So, the O'Ryan party . . ." She turned to her computer. "I'll get you checked in."

"O'Riley," Sean corrected. And why was she playing like she didn't know him? "Lotti, it's me. Sean."

"O'Riley," she repeated, fingers clicking the keyboard. "Yes, here you all are. Twelve guests, two nights. Wine tasting tour tomorrow. Bachelor/bachelorette here tomorrow night. Checking out Sunday morning." She then proceeded to check them in with quick efficiency, managing to avoid Sean's direct gaze the entire time.

It wasn't until she handed him a room key and their fingers touched that she actually met his gaze, her own warm chocolate one clear and startled.

Again she recovered quickly, lifting her chin and turning away.

"You really going to pretend you don't remember me?" he asked quietly.

She didn't answer. This, of course, delighted Finn to no end. He grinned wide at Sean as they all turned to head up the stairs to their rooms.

"What's so funny?" Sean snapped.

"It finally happened. You being put in your place by a woman. And she was hot too."

Pru cuffed Finn upside the back of his head.

"I mean she was smart and funny and had a great personality," Finn said.

Pru rolled her eyes.

"And," Finn went on, "she didn't remember you. That's the best part. Where do you know her from anyway?"

Sean shook his head. "Never mind."

The ass that called himself Sean's brother was still chortling to himself when they all vanished into their respective rooms. Because the B&B had only six guest rooms total, and eight of their group were coupled off, the four singles had been forced to pair up. Sean keyed himself into the room he was going to share with Joe. They both tossed their duffle bags onto each of the two beds.

Twin beds. And shit, those beds were *small*.

Sean stood there hands on hips, the bedding that was thick and comfortable looking, but done up in a girlie floral print, situated *way* too close to Joe's bed to please him.

Joe was looking less than pleased himself. "Damn."

"Yeah. Sucks to be single in a wedding party."

"Yeah," Joe agreed. "But hey, positive spin—it doesn't suck to be single." He flopped onto his bed and grabbed the remote, bringing up an MMA fight.

Sean blew out a breath and turned to the door.

"It's nearly midnight," Joe said to his back. "Where you off to? Back down to the hot chick who didn't recognize you?"

"She totally recognized me," Sean said.

"Right."

"She did."

"Dude, then that's even worse."

Sean flipped him off and left as Joe laughed, heading back down the stairs. Because Joe was right, being recognized and ignored *was* worse. And it was all his own fault.

The night had gotten noisy. Wind battered the old Victorian, rattling the windows, causing the trees outside to brush against the walls, which creaked and groaned under the strain. Sean hoped like hell that the carpenters back in the day had known what they were doing and that the place would hold.

For the second time in ten minutes, he strode up to

the check-in desk. Pru had been the one to insist on this B&B because it'd been built in the late 1800s and had a cool history that he'd been told about in great detail but couldn't repeat to save his life because he hadn't listened. All he knew was that Pru had wanted to stay here so badly that he'd made it happen for her.

But it didn't mean he had to like it.

Lotti was no longer in sight. There was a small bell for service on the desk and just as he reached out to hit it, he heard a male voice from inside what looked to be an office.

"I'm sorry, Charlotte," the unseen man was saying. "But you know we're not working. You're so closed off that I can't get close to you."

Sean froze for two reasons. One, Lotti had always hated her full name. Hated it to the bone so much she'd refused to answer to it.

And two . . . those words. *You're so closed off that I can't get close to you . . .* They reverberated in Sean's head, pulling memories he'd shoved deep. That long-ago summer night they'd shared had been the accumulation of several years of platonic friendship, started when he'd needed help in English and she in chemistry. They'd tutored each other, the perennial bad boy and the perennial good girl, and then one night they'd been each other's world in the back of her dad's pickup on the bluffs of Marin Headlands.

Afterward, she'd told him she loved him. He could remember staring into her sweet eyes and nearly swallowing his own tongue. *Love?* Was that what this all-consuming, heart and gut wrenching emotion he felt for her was? And even though he'd suspected that yes indeed it'd been love, he'd wanted no part of it because it hurt like hell.

And then proving just that, she'd gone on to tell him that her family was moving away, but since they were in love, they could stay in touch and write and call and visit.

She was going to leave. Even with all he'd felt for her, he'd known he wouldn't, couldn't, be the guy she'd needed. She'd indeed written him, and being the chicken-shit, emotionally stunted kid he'd been back then, he hadn't written back. Or returned her calls. Losing her had been like a red-hot poker to the chest but he hadn't been able to see himself in a long-distance relationship, or in any relationship at all.

Hell, he couldn't have committed to a dentist appointment back then.

He'd thought of her, always with a smile and an ache in his chest because he deeply regretted how he'd behaved. By the time he graduated, he'd grown up enough to try to find her to apologize, but he'd had no luck. He'd never seen her again—until now.

A guy came out of the office, presumably the one who'd spoken, and headed straight for the front door, walking out into the storm without looking back.

Sean waited a minute, but there was only silence coming from the office. No sign of Lotti, nor a single sound. Clearly it was the worst possible time to try to talk to her, but her eerie silence worried him.

Then suddenly came the sound of glass shattering, but before he could rush into the room, she came out.

She wasn't crying, which was a huge relief. Her eyes were . . . blank, actually, giving nothing away. That is until she saw Sean. Then they sparked, but not the good kind of spark.

"*You,*" she said.

Yep, he had the bad timing thing down pat.

Chapter Two

OF COURSE SEAN O'RILEY would be the one standing there, witness to the fact that she had a problem letting people in. Gee, wonder where she'd learned such a thing.

Unfortunately, she couldn't turn back time. He'd clearly overheard her being dumped by Trevor, a guy she'd gone out with six and a half times. The half date had been the other night when he'd brought her dinner and had pushed the issue of becoming lovers.

She hadn't been ready and he'd been frustrated with her. She got that, she did, but intimacy was a big—and not easy—step for her and dammit, she'd needed a little more time. Trevor had said he understood, but clearly that hadn't been true. He'd dumped her.

In earshot of her first lover.

Perfect.

And that *that* was her only concern at the moment told her everything she needed to know about her real feelings for Trevor. Clearly, it would never have worked out. Not that this eased her embarrassment one little bit. Honestly, she couldn't see how this night could get any worse and with a sigh, she met Sean's gaze.

And holy cow, an age-old tingle of awareness and heat sliced through her. She decided to attribute this to the fact that he was still sex-on-a-stick, maybe even more so now. Back then he'd been trouble with a capital *T,* but with such charisma that he'd been like the Pied Piper. She'd followed him right to her own undoing.

And she had a feeling not much had changed.

"Is there a problem with your room?" she asked politely, hoping to get rid of him quickly.

But she should've known better. Sean smiled that smile that had once had her panties melting right off. "Yeah," he said. "The bed's too small." He was taller than she remembered and leanly muscled. His hair was still dark but with some lighter streaks from the sun and messily tousled, most likely courtesy of his own restless fingers. His eyes still shined with more mischievousness than any one man should hold.

Not going there, she told herself just as a gust of wind knocked the house like a bolt of lightning. The lights flickered as the electricity surged and she held her breath. This old building could barely tolerate the electrical needs in decades past, so the demands they put on it in the here and now were always a gamble. Luckily the guests they had always seemed charmed if the electricity went out, and she made sure to keep lots of candles and lanterns around. Plus, she had a generator if she needed. But tonight she didn't want any problems. Not when her biggest problem was standing in front of her looking good enough to eat, damn him.

Another gust of wind hit hard and again the electricity blinked on and off again. *Please don't go out, please don't go out . . .*

It went out.

"Are you serious with tonight?" she asked karma or fate, or whoever was in charge of such things.

She heard a rough laugh and then Sean accessed the flashlight on his phone. "This is your fault," she said.

His brows went up and she sighed. "Don't ask me how, it just is. It has to be."

She could see him smiling through the glow. It was that patented bad boy smile and in spite of herself, her heart gave a treacherous little sigh. She hardened both it and her voice. "Thank you," she said with as much dignity as she could muster, leaning on her desk in order to keep her hands off the guy who still had a solo starring role in her every sexual fantasy, and had since high school. A fact she'd take to the grave, thank you very much. And okay, not *every* single fantasy—the Chrises had occasional starring roles as well; Chris Hemsworth, Chris Pine, Chris Pratt . . .

With a sigh, she turned to her desk, a hundred-year-old hand-carved piece, the top inlaid with time-worn leather, the edges rough with life's battle marks. It'd been her father's, a man who'd never wavered in his love for her mom, not once in the thirty years they'd had before he died last year. And yet he'd died of cancer that he hadn't told a soul about, not her mom, not Lotti, no one, nor had he had it treated.

Because that thought led to a dark tunnel that she hadn't yet found a light for, she shook it off and pulled open a desk drawer to grab a Maglite and a box of matches. She'd already had a bunch of candles lit on the mantel so they weren't in the complete dark, but she needed to check on everyone. "I'm sorry, but I don't have a different room to switch you to," she said to Sean. "If you'll excuse me, I need to go check on the other guests."

"It's late," he said. "Everyone's in their rooms. Trust me, they'd come out if they needed something from you."

She cocked her head to listen, but not a soul was moving.

"Not even a mouse," he said with a smile, reading her mind. Then he took her Maglite and beamed it up the stairs. "See? No one. They're all in bed. Tell me what else you need to do, I'll help."

"Hmm," she said.

"And that means . . . ?"

"The last time you 'helped' me, it'd been to remove my jeans," she said, then bit her traitorous tongue. Where had that come from? Oh yeah, it'd come from her very, *very* stupid side.

He winced, like the memories of their past hurt him as much as they did her. Whatever. She wasn't going to be drawn in. She'd lost more than just her virginity that night. She'd lost a chunk of her heart. Not that she wanted it back . . .

Grabbing her flashlight back, she headed for the stairs. "I want to walk the hallway just in case someone needs something." When he followed her, she gave him a long look. "I can handle this."

"Humor me," he said.

So they walked the hallway together, didn't hear a peep out of anyone, and went back downstairs. Because the house was so old, she moved to the front door. She needed to go outside to check the electric panel to see if she'd blown any fuses. She pulled on her jacket and was surprised when she opened the door to find Sean once again coming with her.

He pulled up her hood for her, tucking her hair in, which felt oddly . . . intimate. "You don't have to do this," she yelled. She had to. The wind and rain had whipped up the night so that she could hardly hear her own voice.

"You blame me for this mess. The least I can do is see it through with you."

They ran along the path and around to the side of the house, all while being pelted by the storm. Under the roof's overhang, Lotti stopped, panting for breath. "Here," she said, handing him the flashlight to hold for her so she could pry open the electrical panel. "And I don't really blame you for tonight," she admitted grudgingly to the panel, not wanting to let him off the hook entirely.

Sean moved in closer so that his front brushed her back, protecting her from the worst of the storm with his body. "But you blame me for hurting you, as you should. Trust me, I blame me too. I wish that I'd done things differently."

She closed her eyes against the onslaught of emotions that battered her at his close proximity. "No," she said. "It's not all on you. I wanted you that night. But I do blame you for turning me into a serial monogamist."

He turned her to face him. He'd made sure to pull up her hood, but he didn't have one. His dark hair was drenched and looked midnight black, his way-too-handsome face a perfect backdrop for those startlingly sharp green eyes. "Explain."

"No."

"Try again."

She tossed up her hands. "Fine. You were my first one-night stand and it didn't work out, okay? I mean not even a little! First, it wasn't all that great and second, I thought we were going to be a couple, which you clearly *never* intended. Because of you, I learned to be cautious and careful and became a—"

"—serial monogamist," he repeated, eyes narrowed. "I get it. But back up a second. It wasn't . . . 'all that great'?"

Okay, so she'd totally lied there. She'd thought it might put a halt to this awkward conversation. "This conversation is going to have to get in line behind my other more pressing problems."

"'Wasn't all that great,'" he was echoing to himself. "Yeah, I'm going to need you to explain that."

Oh boy. She wracked her brain for a legitimate gripe. "Well it was over pretty fast and—" She broke off when his eyebrows shot up so far they vanished into his hair.

"It was over pretty fast?" he repeated, so obviously stunned at this tidbit that she had to laugh.

"You're starting to sound like a parrot," she said.

"Just coming to terms with what an asshole I was back then. But in my defense, I was sixteen and pretty stupid."

And grieving. She had to give him that. He'd lost both of his parents in a tragic car accident. At the time, she couldn't imagine the pain he'd been suffering. All she'd wanted to do was take his mind off things.

She was pretty sure she'd done that, at least for a few hours. First, they'd shared some pilfered alcohol, and then he'd kissed her. And oh how good *that* had felt. Until that night, she'd never gone further than a kiss before. Everything Sean had done had turned her on. *Everything*. Until he'd tried to slow her down.

But the alcohol had been like liquid courage and she'd been on the very edge of her first social orgasm. Slowing down hadn't been an option for her and she'd pushed for more. She'd gotten her wish and he'd been sweet and gentle. He'd gone slow, so achingly slow that in the end, she'd been begging him. But they'd been drinking and he hadn't wanted to go all the way. He'd been worried and concerned for her, but she'd pushed the issue, taking the lead, taking him into her body. He'd been buried deep and trembling with the effort to hold back for her when from the front of her dad's truck she'd heard her cell phone going off.

She'd been way past curfew.

It'd been the call to bring her out, to dash her with the proverbial bucket of ice water. The fear of her parents finding out what she'd been up to with "the horrible, rotten, no-good O'Riley boy," and she'd lost her mojo.

Not exactly his fault . . .

"I love you," she'd whispered and she'd never forget the look of panic on his face. She should've suspected it then, but it'd still been such a shock when after she'd moved out of the city he hadn't followed through with his promise about seeing her, not once. With all her ridiculously young heart she'd wanted forever with him. She'd called, written him letters, and she'd poured her heart out in each and every one. He'd never responded and she'd never seen him again.

In hindsight, she knew they'd been far too young for anything serious. They'd both needed more life experiences and maturity. Not that her heart appreciated the reasoning.

"I can promise you," he said, "I've learned a whole lot since then."

The words made certain parts of her anatomy quiver,

which she ignored. "Whatever you say." She turned from him and eyeballed the electrical panel. Just as she thought, she'd blown a fuse. She pulled it out and replaced it with one of the spares she had tucked into the panel for just such incidents.

The electricity came back on.

"Impressive," Sean said.

"What, that a woman might know how to work an electrical panel for her hundred-plus-year-old house?"

"No," he said. "I know how smart you are. I meant it's impressive the lengths you'll go to in order to avoid a real conversation with me."

She blew out a breath. "There's nothing left to talk about."

"I disagree. There's the matter of the 'not that good' thing."

"Oh for God's sake!" She turned to face him. "I take it back, all right? I'll put an ad in craigslist and shout it from the rooftops. Would that make you feel better?"

"No. But getting a chance to make it up to you would."

"In bed, I'm guessing."

"Preferably. But a bed isn't required."

She stared at him and then had to laugh at his audacity. That was all she needed, to get too close and fall for him again. "Pass, but thanks for the offer."

"See," he said. "You *did* mean it."

"Look, I'm sorry if you're insulted by my memory of our one night. But I'm not interested in revisiting it or in having this conversation." She moved around him and dashed back toward the B&B.

With him right behind her.

They stood inside the foyer and did their best to shake off from the rain. Unfortunately, the foyer was small. Too small, and sharing it with him made it seem to shrink even more. She inadvertently brushed against him removing her jacket and another bolt of awareness zinged her.

Back in high school, Sean had been lanky lean, almost to the point of being too skinny. But he'd filled in since then, big time. There was nothing boy-like about him anymore. The Sean she'd known was now *all* man.

Tearing her gaze off of him, she hung up her jacket and couldn't help herself. She dropped her forehead to the wall and banged it a few times. It'd been a long day, and a longer night.

Sean put a hand on her shoulder. "Hey," he said softly. "You okay?"

No, dammit. She wasn't. She lifted her head. "Fine."

"I'm sorry about that ass-munch who dumped you."

She found a laugh. "How do you know he was an ass-munch?"

"Because he called you Charlotte."

She let out another low, rough laugh. Better than tears. "Yes," she said. "Because that's my name."

"You hate being called Charlotte."

"That's what I go by these days."

He held her gaze captive. "Why?"

She shrugged. "It's more professional, I guess. It's a woman's name, not a girl's." She inhaled deeply and managed to keep the eye contact, no easy thing to do. He could charm secrets out of a nun. "No one's called me Lotti in a very long time."

He surprised her by taking a step toward her, closing the already small distance. "I'm sorry if you're hurting," he murmured with a surprising amount of compassion in his voice.

"I'm not." She paused and let out a breath. "At all, actually. Which is the problem."

His gaze never left hers. "I'm still sorry. For a lot of things."

The Sean of old had been a lot of things; wild to the point of being practically feral, as rough and tumble as they came, and *way* too smart for his own good. Deep in his own head because of his grief, what he *hadn't* been was particularly aware of anyone's pain but his own. "Who are you and what have you done with Sean O'Riley?" she asked.

He shrugged. "Maybe you're not the only one who grew up."

She knew that very well could be true, but the odds were against him. And she told herself she didn't care. She had two days left of work and then she was off for two weeks. Two entire weeks! It'd been forever since she'd had any sort of vacation. As in literally forever. She'd gone right from high school to business school, and from business school to running the B&B for her family.

Her mom had happily retired to hand her over the reins and was on a cruise with her sister for the holidays. Lotti didn't have any siblings, though she was as close to her cousin Garrett as she would be a brother. But he wasn't around this Christmas. No one in her family was, so she and her mom had agreed to close the B&B for the next two weeks, allowing Lotti some desperately needed time off. It wasn't a coincidence that she'd picked this time of year. Last Christmas had been a traumatic nightmare what with her dad's passing right before and then getting un-engaged right after.

Lotti didn't just want to get out of town for the holiday, she desperately *needed* to go.

"It's a nice place here," Sean said, looking around. "It suits you, running a B&B."

Why *that* made her want to glow with pleasure, she had no idea. "Thanks. I love it on most days."

His smile was wry, letting her know that he understood today *wasn't* one of those love-it days. Which made her feel a little bit like a jerk. "So what do you do for work?" she asked, genuinely wanting to know more about him. Which was so not good.

He looked a little surprised at the question, which made her feel even worse. "Finn and I own a pub in the city. O'Riley's."

She had to smile. "Talk about a job suiting a person. That sounds perfect for you."

Their gazes met and held and warmth went through her, specifically her good spots, which sent off inner warnings. *Danger, danger . . .* "It's getting pretty late," she said. "I should lock up for the night and go to bed. I'll see you all tomorrow morning for breakfast and then again for the party tomorrow night, as I'll be your server. Then once more Sunday morning when you check out."

He gave her a small smile. "You don't have to look so happy about that last part. Do you have Christmas plans, is that it?"

Sure. That sounded much more logical than the fact that she needed to get far, far away from home and the memories here. "I do."

"Did you make a list and check it twice?"

She had to smile at that. She'd always been extremely organized and a list maker. That he remembered such a thing surprised her. "Yes, I did as a matter of fact. I asked for kittens and rainbows and peace on earth."

"A cynic," he said on a smile. "I didn't see that coming."

She started to laugh but caught herself. "Listen. I don't want you to take this personally," she said. "But I've had a rough year. I've screwed up some pretty big things, I've worked too hard, and I'm tired. But life is short. Too short. I'm going to learn to eat some of the cookies I bake instead of giving them all away to guests. I'm going to read sappy books with happy-ever-after endings instead of book club reads that make me want to kill myself. I'm going to sing in the rain and jump in the puddles no matter what shoes I'm wearing. In fact, I'm going to do it barefoot without worrying about getting a gangrene infection from a cut. I'm going to live life to the fullest, Sean. No regrets."

He studied her for a moment and nodded. "I'm all for that."

"Glad you approve. I'm going on a two-week vacation when you all leave," she said. "I'm going to Cabo. And you can trust me when I say that I've never needed anything more than this trip because . . ." She broke off both speaking and eye contact for a beat, realizing she was revealing far too much. "Well it's a long story."

He looked at her for a moment and she thought maybe he was about to say something, but he seemed to change his mind, instead giving her another small smile.

"I hope it's everything you want it to be," he said and she could tell he meant it.

She nodded and gave him a far more genuine smile than she had before. "Thanks."

TWENTY MINUTES LATER, Lotti lay on her bed in her nine hundred square foot studio apartment above the garage and storage building. Her dad had renovated it for her when she'd come home from college and she loved it. It gave her separation from the B&B, privacy, and yet was a huge convenience if a guest needed anything after hours.

She didn't have much in it; a love seat, her bed, a small kitchen table, and her inheritance from her dad—Peaches the parrot.

"You're late!" Peaches yelled.

She'd forgotten to cover him up for sleep time. She got out of bed and draped a towel over his cage. "Goodnight, Peaches."

"I can still see you!"

Even after nearly a year together, Lotti and Peaches weren't quite yet friends. "Quiet time," she said.

"The meat loaf's dry," Peaches yelled. "You ruined my meat loaf!"

Lotti's dad had thought it was funny to teach Peaches to be a nagging housewife. "Go to sleep."

Peaches sighed and didn't utter another word.

Lotti got back into bed. Her toes and fingers were frozen to the bone as she huddled under the covers warming herself up with thoughts of sandy beaches and endless sun.

She slept deeply and the next day she worked on the accounting books while her guests took a wine tasting tour with Sean as their DD. That had interested her because the Sean of old hadn't been a guy to stand back and let others have all the fun.

But they'd come back with everyone but Sean feeling no pain and she'd had to admit, he appeared to be taking this best man thing seriously. Very seriously. It was . . . attractive, seeing him work hard at making his brother happy.

That night she watched from the sidelines as he ran the bachelor/bachelorette party like he'd been born a host, with natural charm and easy laughter.

And the way the others clearly loved him . . . It made her happy to know that he'd made it, that he'd turned out okay and had so much love and light in his life.

Just as it made her feel slightly alone and a little . . . sad. Because she didn't have that. She had her mom. Her cousin Garrett McGrath. And a few good friends. But her relationships definitely seemed to fall a little short of what Sean had with this group of tight-knit family and friends.

Sunday morning, she woke up before dawn. There was so much to do. She made breakfast, telling herself she was relieved it was check-out day. Soon, Sean would march out of her life again and she'd go to Cabo and forget him.

Okay, so she'd never been able to forget him, but it was past time to learn.

Chapter Three

IT WAS BARELY dawn when Sean sat up in his bed and looked at his phone's notifications. "*Shit.*"

The mound under the covers of the second bed moved. Groaned. Then Joe flopped to his back and gave Sean a bleary-eyed look. "Unless there are two really hot women at our door wanting to jump our bones, it's *way* too early to be up."

"The storm worsened," Sean said. "There's flooding and mudslides up and down the entire state of California. The roads in and out of here are closed."

"Then why the hell are you waking me up?"

"Because mudslides closed Finn and Pru's wedding venue down. Indefinitely."

"Okay, that sucks," Joe said on a wide yawn. "But I think the wedding panic can wait until daylight, yeah?"

And without waiting for an answer, he rolled over and went back to sleep.

Sean dressed and went down the hall, knocking on the first guest room he came to. Tina opened the door. The six-foot-plus dark-skinned goddess was in only a towel, damp from the shower. Behind her, he could see both beds, one tousled but empty, the other holding a sleeping Kylie.

"What's up, Sugar?" Tina asked. "I'm halfway through applying my mascara and it's a process. I need to get back to it."

Sean repeated his spiel. "The storm worsened," he said. "There's mudslides everywhere between here and home. We're not getting out for a while."

Tina smiled. "A few extra days away from the city and work? Love it."

"The wedding venue closed."

"Well damn," Tina said. "But we'll help Pru and Finn figure it out. Later, when I have all my lashes on."

Behind Tina, Kylie sat up, looking confused. Her hair was rioted all around her head as she narrowed her eyes at Sean. "Why are you interrupting my beauty sleep?"

"The weather—"

"—Sean," she said, holding up a hand. "I love you. I do. But this bed's amazing. In fact, I plan to marry the next guy that makes me feel even half as good as this bed does. So please go away."

Sean moved to the next door. Neither Archer nor Elle bothered to answer to his knock so he texted Archer.

Sean: It's me. Open up.

Archer: Keep knocking and die. Painfully.

Okay then. Since Archer wasn't much of a joker, Sean kept moving. But at Spence and Colbie's room, it was more of the same, although they at least answered the door. Both had clearly been otherwise preoccupied. Spence told Sean not to expect him and Colbie until much, *much* later.

Giving up on riling anyone else up besides himself, Sean made his way downstairs. He sat at one of the three round dining room tables. The power had gone out again and stayed off this time, so the only light came from a few well-placed lanterns and candles. He checked his phone but nothing had changed.

They were still screwed.

In fact, most of Northern California was, and now also in a newly declared state of emergency. Overnight there'd been three inches of rain causing mudslides, sinkholes, and massive road closures. People couldn't get out of Napa Valley. And they couldn't get *into* Napa Valley—not that that mattered with the wedding venue closed down. It'd be months, their site said, before they recovered from the devastating mudslides and were operating again.

"It's a nightmare," Finn said, plopping down next

to him. He had a plate full of food from the sideboard buffet.

Sean slid his gaze to his brother as he shoved in some French toast and bacon. "Real upset over it, are you?"

"Devastated," Finn said and craned his neck to eyeball the food platters. "Think we can go back up there for seconds?"

"Are you serious?"

"Yeah. The French toast's amazing here. That innkeeper, Lotti? She's incredible. She's got a small generator and she used it to cook for us. Have you eaten yet?"

"No," Sean said. "I haven't. Because I've been sitting here trying to figure out how to save your wedding. Where's Pru?"

"She and the girls are about to go have mimosas in the thankfully gas-powered hot tub."

Sean stared at him. "Does she know about the flooding and mudslides closing down her wedding venue?"

"Yep."

"And she's okay?"

"No," Finn said. "Which is why she's inhaling alcohol at the asscrack of dawn. Listen, she's trying to have a good attitude about this and so am I." He shoved in more French toast. "She said as long as we're in the same place with the people we love, that's good enough. I have to believe her. She waited a long time for this and now there's nothing else open all year. We might have to hit up the courthouse to tie the knot and throw a party. Whatever she wants." Finn wolfed down the rest of his food and sighed, scrubbing a hand down his face, revealing his tension and stress.

For years the guy had been taking care of Sean. When their parents had died, Sean had been a fourteen-year-old punk-ass kid, but Finn hadn't hesitated. At twenty-one, he'd stepped into the role of mom and dad and brother, and for a lot of days also judge and jury and jailer.

He'd never once failed Sean.

But Sean had failed Finn. Way too many times to count. He owed Finn everything, including the fact that he was even still here to tell the tale, because there'd been more than a few times where his stupidity should've gotten him killed.

And during that time, Finn hadn't once given up on him. He hadn't even let Sean see the strain it'd surely taken on his own life, taking care of a perpetually pissed-off-at-the-world teenager.

But this, today . . . it was a strain. It was in the tightness of Finn's shoulders and the grim set to his mouth.

His older brother wasn't okay.

And Sean was going to have his back, no matter what. He clasped a hand on Finn's shoulder. "I'm going to work this out for you guys," he said.

Finn smiled and shook his head. "Not your problem, man. Don't worry about it."

Something Finn had been saying to Sean since day one. *Don't worry about it, I'll handle it.* And he had. No matter what Sean had thrown at him.

Finn got to his feet.

"Where are you going?" Sean asked.

"To join my hopefully soon-to-be wife in the hot tub."

"Finn, we still have to check out of here this morning."

Finn shook his head. "You said it yourself, the roads are closed. We're not going anywhere."

"Did anyone actually check in with Lotti about the fact that we have to extend our stay?"

Finn stopped. "Shit. No."

"Don't worry about it," Sean said. "I'll handle it." And with that, he got up and moved out to the front room to deal with the problems for once.

There was no sign of Lotti at the front desk so he walked around it and peered into her office, hitting the jackpot.

Lotti was in the corner, sitting on top of a very over-stuffed suitcase, bouncing up and down on it trying to get it closed while simultaneously listening to a call she had on speaker.

A female voice was saying ". . . I can't believe you talked me into this, a cruise through the Greek islands with Aunt Judie, but we're having a ball, honey. I just want you to remember your promise to me before I left, that you're going to use your honeymoon tickets and go to Cabo. You need a breather from the past year, first losing your daddy and then breaking off your wedding—"

"Mom." Lotti closed her eyes. "I'm fine."

"Are you?"

"Yes," Lotti said firmly. "I mean, I did wake up this morning to realize I'm still not a billionaire rock star rocket scientist martial arts master, but hey, it could be worse, right?"

"Honey. I worry about you. If you don't leave your past in the past, it'll destroy your future. You've got to live for what today's offering, not for what yesterday took away from you."

"You sound like a Hallmark card."

"They don't make cards for this, Lotti."

"I'm okay, Mom. Really," Lotti said firmly. "Tell me about you."

"Well . . . are you ready for this? I'm wearing sunscreen and a very cute new dress that I couldn't pair a bra with, and there's a gentleman who keeps sending me drinks. I think I'm about to have a very good time."

"Be safe," Lotti said softly. "Love you."

"Love you too!"

Lotti tapped the screen of her phone and disconnected. Then she looked down at the suitcase beneath her and sighed before going back to bouncing on it to try to get it zipped. "Come on you, fu—"

"Here," Sean said, coming into the office to crouch in front of her, taking over possession of the zipper. "Let me."

Lotti had gone Bambi in the headlights. "Where did you come from?" she asked.

"Well when a mommy and daddy love each other very much they—"

"Were you eavesdropping?" she demanded, not amused.

"No."

"So . . . you heard nothing?" she asked suspiciously. "Nothing at all?"

He lifted his attention from the suitcase that was not going to zip and met her gaze.

She searched his face and closed her eyes. "Dammit."

He put a hand on her leg. "I'm sorry—"

"No. You don't get to say that to me."

"I lost my dad too, Lotti. And my mom. No one understands how that feels except someone who's been through it."

She chewed on that for a minute. Trying to get her emotions under control, he realized.

"Are you also going to tell me that you've been dumped by a fiancé a week before your wedding?" she finally asked.

"Well no, but—"

"No buts." She shoved his hand from her. "I don't want to talk about it."

"Lotti—"

"Ever," she said firmly. "New subject."

"Okay. How about the fact that there's no way your suitcase is going to close."

"Dammit." She hopped off the suitcase and kneeled in front of it, pulling out some of the clothes. "I tried to pack light. But it was hard to decide on what to wear . . ."

"Depends on what you want to get out of the trip," he said.

She bit her lower lip and blushed, and he went brows up. "Ah," he said. "You want to get laid."

"No," she said but even her ears were deep red now.

"Hey, there's nothing wrong with that," he said.

She met his eyes and then rolled hers. "Well gee, thanks for the permission." She pulled something else from her suitcase and held it up to herself. A white strappy sundress. "Would this dress make you want me?"

He had to laugh. "Lotti, when I first met you, you were in PE class wearing a baggy T-shirt and sweats and I wanted you."

"I'm being serious, Sean."

"So am I."

She shook her head. "Back then was a lot of years ago and I'm not that same skinny kid. Be honest, is the dress too much? I don't want to look desperate, even though I am."

"The dress is perfect," he said, not liking that she believed she needed the dress to attract a man. All she needed to do was lay those heart-stopping eyes on someone and it'd be over. All the rest; her smile, her brain, her bod . . . it was all gravy. "On second thought," he said and snatched the sundress and tossed it aside.

She snorted and tried again to get the zipper closed, bouncing up and down on the suitcase again. "Is this helping?"

Sean tried not to watch her lovely breasts jiggle and failed. "Helps a lot."

She followed his gaze to her chest and snorted again. "You're impossible."

He got the suitcase closed and rose to his feet to help her to hers. "Just trying to take your mind off your troubles." And he meant that. He wanted to take her mind off the phone call, something he himself couldn't do.

She'd been left by her fiancé.

Her dad had died.

And she'd needed this Cabo getaway more than he'd known. "I'm sorry about today, Lotti."

Startled, her dark eyes met his. "What about it?"

"Well, for starters, about us not checking out—"

"Oh, you don't have to check out," she said. "It's automatic. All you have to do is leave."

"Yeah, about that . . . Have you checked the news or weather?"

She stared at him and then shook her head. "Not yet. I got sidetracked trying to get my suitcase closed."

"We can't leave, Lotti."

"Sure you can," she said. "You just get in your vehicle and go." She gave him a little push toward the door for emphasis. "Okay, then. Thanks for coming, buh-bye . . ."

But Sean wasn't walking away. Not that this stopped her from trying to get him to. She put her hands on his chest and pushed again. It seemed to take her a second to realize that he wasn't going to be moved. Finally, she went hands on hips and gave him a long look. "You're leaving, and so am I. I've got big plans."

Yeah, he knew. Plans that had nearly involved the sexy white sundress he couldn't get his mind off of.

"I mean it," she said. "I'm heading straight to the airport and Cabo. So if you're about to give me any sort of news to the contrary, I don't want to hear it."

She was spoiling for a fight, but he wasn't going to give it to her, not with that vulnerable look on her face and his realization that she needed this get away so much more than he'd even realized. "I'm sorry," he said quietly. "I really am. But you need to bring up your flight app. Or your weather or news app."

She looked out the window where the rain and wind had actually died down for the time being. "Why? What don't I know?"

"The highways are closed."

Her head whipped back to face him. "What?"

"Which means people can't get out," he said. "People like us. And you."

"No."

"Yes."

She stared at him and let out a long, shuddering breath. "Okay, you know what? After much consideration, I've decided adulthood isn't for me. Thank you and goodbye."

"I'm sorry, Lotti."

"No, you don't understand," she said. "I have flights."

"I know."

She looked around. "And I'm actually off work for once. There's no other guests until after the first of the year." She paused. "Are you sure there aren't any open roads out of here, not a single one?"

"Not until the storm moved on and they've cleared everything of debris. The reports say we're at least twenty-four hours out from that. More likely forty-eight hours, or even more."

"Oh my God." She sank heavily to her desk chair, dropping her forehead to the desk. "This is all my fault."

"Yeah? You personally called Mother Nature and asked her to unload her wrath?"

Keeping her head down, she moaned. "I actually thought this was going to happen, that I could get away from here. Two weeks, that's all I asked for."

"I'm so sorry your vacay got screwed up. And I'm sorry for my next question."

She lifted her head. Her smile faded. "Sean, you can't stay. I'm closing down the inn."

"That's already happened, Lotti," he said on a low laugh. "I hear you but there's literally nowhere to go."

With a sigh, she stood up and faced him. "Okay, then what's your question?"

"Since we're all stuck for at least the next twenty-four hours, I was hoping we could throw my brother and Pru an impromptu wedding reception."

"That's usually preceded by an actual wedding," she said.

"Yeah. Thought we could do that too."

She stared at him. "You've lost it."

"This place is actually the perfect wedding setting."

She laughed but when he didn't, she shook her head. "Sean, a wedding is an organized event. I mean, I'm a very organized person. I have lists and check them twice and all that, but even I couldn't pull this off on the fly on my own, and I don't have any employees scheduled because I was supposed to be off work." She picked up a clipboard on her desk and showed him, flipping through all the stuff she had on it.

She was right, she was organized as hell. He stopped her on the page labeled: Cabo. There were three things listed:

> Sand
>
> Surf
>
> Surfer

"That's my to do list for Cabo," she said. "Beneath it's my flight itinerary, which says nothing about being sidelined by the storm of the century."

He met her gaze, which was dialed to stubborn and determined. And . . . hopeful. "Your to do list includes a surfer?" he asked.

She looked a little embarrassed but held his gaze. "I've discovered that I've got a little problem with relationships," she said. "So I'm trying something new. I'm going for the *opposite* of a relationship. And nothing, not the storm, not my B&B responsibilities, not even you is going to stop me."

"I can appreciate that," he said. "But—"

"No buts, Sean. I don't have time for buts. And here, let me make you another list, one of everything else I don't have time for." She grabbed a pen and hurriedly scribbled on a piece of paper, which she handed to him.

Things I don't have time for:

1. Your shit
2. Crazy shit
3. Bullshit
4. Stupid shit
5. Fake shit
6. Shit that has nothing to do with me

He laughed, thinking his younger self had been the biggest idiot on the planet that he'd let her get away. She was funny, sweet, amazing, and sexy as hell. "I get it," he said. "But sometimes life doesn't play along. We're not getting out of here and neither are you."

"Dammit," she said.

"So . . . about having a wedding here . . ."

"Seriously, you're nuts."

Yeah. There was no doubt. And something else. He couldn't stop looking at her. For him, she was everything he'd never deserved, especially all those years ago. He should've left things alone, left their attraction as a "what if." But he'd never been good at leaving things alone. He hadn't been able to resist taking a taste of her, even though he'd not been mature enough for her. He'd had issues over losing people, big issues.

So when she'd told him that she was moving, he'd

simply walked away first. Yeah, he'd been a first-rate asshole, but the truth was he always walked first to protect himself.

Except now the joke was on him because even to this very day, she was still the one who'd gotten away. And as a result of what he'd done, Lotti now walked away from relationships, at least emotionally, because she was afraid of getting hurt and he hated that. "It's not *completely* nuts," he said. "I could get ordained online and—"

"Sean," she said on a low laugh. "It won't work. There's not enough room, for one thing. And there's no one to cater. No wedding decorations or cake or—"

"The big living room is perfect," he said. "We all fit in it, no problems. And you won't have to do a thing, I'll handle it all."

She just stared at him. "That doesn't sound like you."

He managed a small smile. "People change, Lotti. I've changed."

"So you keep saying," she said softly and paused. "Look, I think it's incredibly sweet of you to want to do this for your brother. You're trying to make up for your past."

He held her gaze. "Yes. Apparently, I have a lot to make up for."

She flushed a pretty pink and lifted a shoulder.

"Oh, don't go shy on me now," he said with a smile. "I still need to hear specifics on the 'not that great' thing."

She covered her face.

He felt a ping in his heart. "I really was that bad, huh?" he said as lightly as he could.

"Well, it's not like I'm keeping score or anything," she murmured demurely.

"But . . ." he coaxed, giving her a "go on" gesture with his hand.

"Okay, okay, but remember you asked." She hesitated. "Everything was actually great, but only one of us . . . finished."

He winced at his own ineptitude back then but managed to catch her when she laughed and went to turn away. "If I could go back," he said solemnly, "and do things differently, I would."

This clearly surprised her. "You would?"

"One hundred percent." He paused. "I'd like a chance to right my wrongs with you, Lotti. *All* of them."

She stared up at him as if she wanted to believe that and he leaned in, letting their bodies touch, and when her breath caught, he felt a surge of relief.

He wasn't in this alone. She still felt something for him, even if she didn't know what exactly.

"I think you'll be too busy to right that particular wrong," she said a little breathlessly, not moving away, but instead making sure they stayed plastered up against each other.

He stared down at her mouth and wanted it on his. So badly that he lost track of what she was saying. "Too busy doing what?"

"Giving your brother a wedding."

"Wait." He stilled. "You're in?"

"Well far be it for me to be the one who stands in the way of you doing something amazing for your brother," she said. "Besides, what do you know about planning a wedding?"

"Uh..."

"Exactly," she said. "I'm going to go out on a limb here and guess that you know *nothing* about it. Whereas I know more than you, at least. So..."

"So..." He took her hand in his. "We're doing this."

She inhaled a deep breath and let it out slowly as she squeezed his hand. "I guess I'm nuts too, but yeah, we're doing this."

Chapter Four

LOTTI WAS PRETTY good at picking herself back up after a fall, proverbial or otherwise. She'd had to be. By late afternoon, the storm had renewed itself and she'd resigned herself to that, and also to playing hostess for longer than she'd intended. And if she was being honest, it wasn't exactly a hardship to get an extra day or two with Sean in the house.

Darkness came quick at this time of year. In one blink, the gray and stormy day turned to a pitch black stormy night. Electricity had come and gone several times.

They were all pretty much used to it by now.

Lotti had spent several hours with everyone, going over what they could do to make a wedding actually work. Lotti had been pleasantly surprised to find Pru a very calm, logical, easy to please bride-to-be. Sean's brother, Finn, was pretty great too. He just wanted to make Pru happy.

The rest of the friends were . . . well, amazing. Flexible. Loving. Sarcastic. Lotti loved them all. They'd decided on the next day for the ceremony and were making lists for the plans.

"I'm so excited we're going to do this here," Pru's friend Willa said. "It was going to be a 'rustic Christmas' wedding at the winery, but this here . . ." She gestured to the holiday-decoration-strewn place. "This is the real deal rustic. And also, you're wonderful, Lotti. And you too, Pru. If the weather had messed up *my* wedding, I'd probably be acting like an angel who'd just had their wings broken."

"We're *all* angels," Elle, another bridesmaid, said. "And when someone breaks our wings, we simply continue to fly . . . on a broomstick. We're flexible like that."

"We're extremely limited in food and resources," Lotti warned. "I was expecting to close up today for several weeks so supplies are almost nonexistent."

Finn looked worried about this. "You mean food? We're short food?"

Pru, sitting next to him, raised a brow. "Since when do we need food to get married?"

"We need sustenance, that's all I'm saying. Maybe—"

"Hold on." Pru gave him a long look. "If you're trying to say you don't want to do this after talking me into it, then let me be clear and say that I *will* run you through with my umbrella while you sleep."

Finn blinked. "That was oddly specific and violent."

"I stand by my statement," Pru said.

Finn eyed said umbrella and nudged it farther away from her.

Pru laughed before looking around the room at her friends, all of whom were sitting around, taking part in this emergency wedding meeting. "I know we could wait," she said. "I could start all over with a new venue, but . . . I don't want to." She reached for Finn's hand. "Everyone we love and need is right here. I want to do this. Here."

Finn leaned over, and apparently not at all concerned about their audience, kissed her softly. He stayed close, their gazes connected for a long beat during which their love seemed to fill the room.

It was so . . . *real* that Lotti actually had to look away. She'd never experienced anything like what the two of them shared, had never in her life yearned that much for one person. Her gaze collided with Sean's and her heart skipped a beat. Okay, so she had felt that way. Once. But she'd been young and stupid. It'd been puppy love, clearly not anything like what Pru and Finn so clearly had. But now she could admit that after only a few days with Sean as an adult, he was even more appealing than he'd been all those years ago and looking into his green eyes, she saw emotion there, deep emotion.

I want a chance to right my wrongs with you, Lotti. All of them.

Damn but he still could still reach her. In the gut. In her overactive brain. And the hardest hit was . . . right in her heart, and she had to close her eyes and remind herself she no longer was interested in such things. Not even a little bit. She'd already planned to go the opposite route from here on out and she needed to stick with that. Sun, surf, surfer.

She realized everyone was looking at her and that Pru had asked a question. "I'm sorry," she said. "What did you say?"

"I just wanted to make sure you're really okay with all this," Pru said. "It's asking an awful lot of you. We're of course going to pay for everything; the extra stay, your time, your resources, all of it. But . . . are you really okay with us pretty much hi-jacking your B&B and turning it into a wedding site?"

"Of course," Lotti said with much more ease than she felt, avoiding Sean's gaze because he seemed to still be able to read her like a book. "We're already halfway there."

Pru nodded and reached over and hugged her. "Thank you."

"What will you wear?" Elle asked.

Pru's smile fell a bit. "Oh crap. I don't have a dress. I never even thought of that."

"I have a dress," Lotti said and when everyone looked at her, she lifted a shoulder. "Don't worry, it was never worn. We've done weddings here before, in the backyard. There's also a pretty wooden archway in the shed out back. And I have those beautiful potted flowers in the dining room and foyer. We can rearrange them in here to make an aisle."

Everyone was looking at her in awe like she was some sort of creative genius. But she wasn't. Not even close. It'd all been for *her* wedding, the one that hadn't actually happened. But hell, it might as well all go to some good, right?

Right.

By that night, Lotti was looking down at her clipboard thinking they might actually pull this off. The property next door belonged to a rancher who'd been the son of her dad's best friend. Jack told her to send someone over, that he could help with extra provisions. On the far side of him was another neighbor, Sally, a close friend who ran a garden nursery. She said she didn't have much in the way of blooming flowers at this time of year but to come over and help themselves.

Lotti had sent the guys to the ranch and the ladies to the nursery. Everyone came back wet but the men had three frozen pizzas, a package of bacon, and the makings for tacos. Lotti slid a worried look to Pru on the items but she seemed on board.

"I know some people are all about live, laugh, love," Pru said. "But I'm all about pizza, bacon, and tacos."

During the cleaning and straightening and planning melee, Lotti's mom called to check on her since she'd seen the weather on the news. Lotti had told her she was fine, she still had guests and was working.

Her mom had paused. "Anyone single and gainfully employed and worth going for?"

Lotti had rolled her eyes and then rushed her off the phone before being dragged into that conversation, because her mom had *nothing* on the CIA. She could sniff out a secret from five thousand miles no problem.

Not ten minutes later, Lotti's phone buzzed an incoming text from her cousin Garrett.

Garrett: You didn't get to Cabo.

Lotti: Mom's such a tattletale. Weather's bad.

Garrett: She didn't say anything about the weather. She had hopes you were with a guy.

Lotti: Is there a point to this conversation?

Garrett: Just remember, if his name starts with A-Z, he's likely to ruin your life. You were warned.

Lotti had to laugh, but she put her phone away and her family out of her mind. That night, they all shared the pizzas, saving the bacon for the morning and the tacos for the wedding feast. Afterward, everyone went to bed early.

With the storm still battering the poor house, Lotti stood in the living room and took in the big picture windows and wide open wooden staircase, knowing that it'd make a beautiful spot for a wedding. One that would actually happen . . .

She drew in a deep breath and wondered what had come over her to agree to such madness. She had no idea.

Except she did. In spite of herself and the things she'd been through, she still believed in love.

And . . . she wasn't quite ready to have Sean walk away. Not yet. The thought gave her a hot flash. Needing some fresh air, she walked through the kitchen and stepped out the back door, stopping under the roof overhang, listening to the rain fall as she took in the view of the valley. Dressed in a light sweater, skirt, and tights, she wasn't exactly prepared for the weather but she didn't care.

A few minutes later, someone joined her on the patio. Sean.

He met her gaze, studied her face as if he was making sure she was okay, and when he realized she was, he gave her a small smile. They stood there together, neither speaking, standing side by side as the rain fell. When their fingers brushed against each other, Sean turned his hand, touching his palm to hers, entwining their fingers.

"You were amazing today," he said. "I can't believe how you put an entire wedding together in one day."

She shrugged, hoping to keep her secrets to herself. She felt the weight of Sean's gaze on her face and she closed her eyes so he couldn't catch her thoughts like only he seemed to be able to do, but she was too late.

"Lotti," he said softly. Just that. Just her name, with a whole lot of feeling in it.

Shit. He knew. She swallowed hard and stared out into the night—until he turned her to face him.

"Lotti," he said again, that same level of emotion in his voice.

"Don't," she whispered.

"I'm sorry," he said huskily. "I should've seen it earlier. All this . . . it was for your wedding."

"Well not the pizzas."

He didn't smile. "I hate that I put you in this position. It's not too late, Lotti. You don't have to do this."

"It's okay. Really." She closed her eyes. "But I'd like to be alone now."

"I get that, and I'd really like to give you what you want," he said. "But I can't. Not this time."

Chapter Five

AT THE EMPATHETIC tone in Sean's voice, Lotti's heart and stomach and head all clenched in unison. "What do you mean you can't give me what I want?" she asked. "All you have to do is walk away."

"Tried that already," he said. "And it was the biggest mistake of my life." He brought her hand up to his mouth and met her gaze over their entwined hands.

He was looking at her like . . . well, she wasn't sure what was going on in his head, but *her* thoughts were racing along with her pulse.

"You're incredible, Lotti. I hope you know that." Very slowly, clearly giving her time to object, he pulled her into him.

Her breath caught at the connection and his eyes heated in response as he slid a hand up her spine and then back down again, pressing her in tight to him from chest to thighs and everywhere in between. His nose was cold at the crook of her neck, but his breath was warm against her skin. She felt his lips press against the sensitive spot just behind her ear and she shivered. "You're trembling," he said, his voice low. "Are you cold?"

"No," she whispered. Try the opposite of cold . . .

"Nervous?"

"No." Not even close. The way his mouth moved across her skin was making her warm all over. Not that she could articulate that with his body pressed to hers and his fingers dancing over her skin. She was literally quivering as the memories of what it felt like to be touched by him washed over her, as if no time at all had gone by.

Yes, she'd let him think that their time together had sucked for her. But it hadn't. Not even close. That long-ago night he'd evoked feelings and a hunger in her that she'd never forgotten. "I've just had a long day," she said.

"I know. I'm going to make it better." He pressed a kiss at the juncture of her jaw and ear before he made his way to her lips for a slow, hot kiss, his mouth both familiar and yet somehow brand-new. She was so far gone that when he pulled back she protested with a moan, but he held her tight, staring down at her with heated eyes. "Just checking," he murmured.

"Checking what?"

"That you want this as badly as I do."

She sure as hell hadn't meant to want him at all, but she fisted her hands in his shirt and yanked him back in.

When he let out a soft laugh, she kissed him to shut him up. She shut herself up too as she lost herself in his kiss, in his touch as their hands grappled to get on each other, touching, caressing, possessing.

She'd have denied this until her dying day, but God she'd missed this, missed the feel of his mouth on hers, missed his hands on her body, missed *him*.

But she was no longer a clueless teenager, and neither was Sean. They were grownups with entirely different lives from each other. "I can't," she whispered and slowly opened her eyes to face his.

"Can't?" he asked. "Or not interested?"

She hesitated, but then gave a slow shake of her head. "Not interested."

Sean gave her fingers—the ones she'd dug into his biceps—a wry look.

She quickly dropped her hands. Okay, fine. She was interested. So very interested. And also dying of curiosity. Would this time feel different?

"I've changed," he promised her. "Give me a chance, Lotti. Give us a chance."

Unable to help herself, she touched his jaw, letting her fingers slide into his silky hair and for a beat, pressed close to him again. It'd be so easy to fall for him. *Too* easy. And knowing it, she stepped back. "I've changed too," she said. "No more relationships for me. They don't work out."

"How many?"

She blinked. "How many what?"

"How many relationships haven't worked out?" he asked.

"Two, an ex-boyfriend and ex-fiancé."

"You're not counting me?"

"Hard to count someone you only got naked with one time."

He paused and then laughed softly. Mad, she turned away to go back inside but he caught her and pulled her around. He'd stopped laughing, which meant she didn't have to kill him outright, but he was still smiling.

"I don't appreciate you laughing at me," she said stiffly.

"I'm not laughing at you," he said. "You're amazing. I'm laughing at myself. We've *both* been relationship shy. You, because I hurt you. Me, because I'm the idiot who hurt you. Please give me another chance, Lotti."

She shook her head. "No. I'm over that. I'm going to Cabo to drink fancy cocktails and smell like coconut sunscreen and to have a one-night stand with *no* strings."

He stared down into her eyes, no longer laughing. Or smiling. "I know I have no right to ask, but do you trust me, even a little?"

"I don't know." She stared at him right back. "Maybe a very little tiny spark."

"I'll take that." He gave her a quick kiss that was no less heart-stopping than his previous one. "Give me fifteen minutes. I'll meet you at your apartment."

"For what?"

But he was already gone.

You're not going to do it, she told herself. No way. She hadn't been expecting him. At all. In fact, many times over the years she'd told herself to forget him.

But she hadn't. Not even a little bit.

Chapter Six

FIFTEEN MINUTES LATER Lotti climbed the stairs to her apartment.

"You're late!" Peaches yelled as she entered.

She ignored the parrot for a moment, Sean's earlier words floating in her brain.

Do you trust me, even just a little?

She still wasn't sure but her apartment was lit with candles flickering on every surface. He'd somehow come up with two large cutouts of palm trees, which were on either side of her bed. There were blue and green scarves on top of her lampshades, giving the entire place the feel of . . . water.

Sean stood in the center of the room wearing board shorts and a T-shirt that advertised some surf shop in Mexico. No shoes and a pair of sunglasses shoved up on his head. He was holding a pitcher of what looked like strawberry margaritas and a bottle of coconut suntan oil.

"What's all this?" she asked.

"Take out the trash!" Peaches yelled.

Sean slid a look at the parrot. "We discussed this," he told the bird. "You were going to let me do the talking."

"All you want is sex!" Peaches squeaked. "I need it to mean something!"

Lotti strode across the room, took a blue silk scarf off one of the lamps, and covered Peaches's cage. "Say goodnight, Peaches."

"Goodnight, Peaches," Peaches muttered and huffed out a sigh.

Lotti turned to Sean, who was laughing. "I didn't train him," she said. "My dad did. He wanted to drive my mom crazy." She took in the room and realized he'd incorporated everything she'd had on her clipboard. Sand, surf . . . surfer. And he was most definitely the hottest surfer she'd ever seen. "What is all this, Sean?"

"Since you can't get to Mexico, I brought Mexico to you."

"How did you accomplish all this in fifteen minutes?"

"Maybe you're not the only one with the taking care of everyone else skill." He lifted a shoulder with a little self-deprecating grimace. "Mine, of course, is a newer skill, so I'm not sure how I'm doing."

Her heart squeezed. "You're doing amazing." And

because the answering look he gave her had more than her heart reacting, she went for a distraction. "Tell me that's strawberry margaritas."

"It is. And I didn't do this alone. I had help. Elle, Pru, Willa, and Colbie are real good in a pinch. Especially Elle. She's a miracle maker. We're not even sure she's human." He poured them each a glass—hers had a little umbrella in it. He gently clicked his drink to hers. "To Mexico."

She drank to that and then rolled her sore neck.

He gently took her glass and set it on her nightstand. "Take off your sweater and lie down," he said. "On your front."

She went brows up. "I don't think I've had enough tequila yet."

"I'm going to use the suntan oil for all your kinks."

Her breath stuttered in her throat as all sorts of dirty, wicked images floated in her head.

". . . In your neck," he said with a smile that said he knew exactly where her mind had gone.

She'd reached for her drink and taken a big sip when he'd said "kinks," and she nearly snorted tequila out her nose. "I'm not losing my top before you do," she wheezed.

Without a word, he pulled his T-shirt off and let it hit the floor. He stood there looking comfortable as hell in nothing but those board shorts riding low on his hips, revealing proof that the lean, lanky boy was now all man. Still lean but oh so many muscles, each delineated in a way that was making her mouth water. She took another gulp of her liquid courage. "You really think I'm just going to strip?"

"That would be my greatest fantasy, but all I asked for was your sweater."

She took another long sip of her margarita. "Okay," she said, staring at his chest, the one she wanted to lick like a lollipop from his chin to waistband of those shorts and beyond. "Just my sweater." But she didn't move.

He smiled. "It's not like I haven't seen it all before."

"Hey, that was a long time ago!"

He cocked his head, looking her over. "Has anything changed?"

"No." Well, maybe a little. She wasn't as skinny as she'd been, for one thing. "Maybe," she admitted.

"I'll close my eyes."

She snorted again and pulled off her top. Beneath she was wearing a plain black sports bra. Not exactly sexy since it had more coverage than a bathing suit top would've provided. Feeling safe, she climbed up on her bed and lay facedown. "Do your worst."

The scent of coconut hit her just before his warm hands did. Coated in oil, they glided firmly up her back and she let out a shuddery moan of pleasure before she could stop herself.

It'd been so long since someone had touched her . . . too long. She wanted him to keep going, wanted him to touch every inch of her and remind her what she'd been missing.

She felt the depression of the mattress when Sean got

onto the bed and straddled her for a better reach. Then his amazing hands went to work kneading the knots in her shoulders and neck, and she moaned again.

"You're a mess, baby," he murmured, his fingers tangling with her sports bra.

She *was* a mess and in far more ways than one. Reaching back, she unhooked the bra's three hooks and Sean stilled.

Buoyed by that, Lotti went through the acrobatic motions of carefully pulling her arms out of the loops without revealing too much or showing him her face, which she knew would've been the biggest reveal of all. She was sure her need and hunger was all over it.

"Lotti." Sean's voice sounded strained, husky, and she felt herself go damp in response.

"Wouldn't want to get funny tan lines," she said.

He let out a low half laugh, half groan, and then his weight shifted. "Tan lines are a bitch," he agreed. He was at her side again, this time so his hands could glide beneath her skirt. He got ahold of her tights and slid them down her legs, dropping them to the floor.

Now *she* was the one to freeze. Not because she wanted him to stop but because she was afraid he *would* stop. She felt his coconut oiled hands on her legs now, massaging his way up from the balls of her feet to the backs of her thighs, just under the edge of her skirt.

"Lotti?" he asked, voice gruff.

She had to clear her throat to speak. "Yeah?"

"How do you feel about tan lines on your ass?"

"Hate them," she said.

Her skirt was gone before she could blink. By some miracle, she was wearing her favorite pair of purple bikini bottoms.

"Pretty," he murmured. "But they've got to go too." And then he hooked his thumbs on either side and slowly pulled them down. They hit the floor by her skirt and she held her breath.

As if she wasn't laid out before him like some sort of feast, he started at the bottom of her feet again, slowly working his strong fingers over the tense muscles. Her calves. The backs of her thighs. Her lower back. Her upper back, shoulders, and neck. Her arms, all the way down to her fingers. And then finally, he made his way down her spine to her ass.

Until now, he'd been silent, giving her the best massage of her entire life. If she hadn't been so unbearably aroused, she might have fallen asleep. But as he went along, he mixed in a series of knowing touches that had her on the very edge. He stroked the tips of his fingers along her ribs and the sides of her breasts, the tops of the back of her thighs, making sure to graze her butt here and there too.

When he cupped a cheek in each of his big palms and squeezed, kneading, spreading her open, he let out a rough groan at the view he gave himself.

"Spread your legs, baby," he said softly, and then did it himself. With a hand on each of her ankles, he nudged her legs apart. Then he was between them, going back to massaging her again while she writhed helplessly beneath him, so unbearably aroused she couldn't lie still. Her nipples rubbed against her blanket, the same blanket that was balled up at the vee of her thighs, teasing her halfway to an orgasm. "Sean—"

"Turn over," he said, his voice giving her a full body shiver, which was when she realized it wasn't the blankets at all. It was 100 percent him.

Chapter Seven

LOTTI HAD A choice. Call this off now, or turn over and take what she wanted—which happened to be one sexy as hell Sean O'Riley.

She turned over.

Sean's dark eyes went molten lava and his breath caught audibly. "You're the most beautiful thing I've ever seen," he said and it was crazy. Just his words now, with neither of his hands on her, had her squirming.

In the ambient lighting he'd created, he looked like a pagan god, leaning over her in nothing but those board shorts, now so low on his lean hips as to be nearly indecent. She'd never seen anything sexier in her entire life. Catching her staring, he smiled and went to pour more oil on his hands but she shook her head.

"One of us is overdressed," she murmured.

Setting down the oil, he rose and unfastened his board shorts. Letting them fall, he kicked them off.

He'd gone commando and was aroused. Very aroused. She moistened her dry lips and said, "I'm glad I'm not on curfew this time. I don't think I can take another interruption."

Another low laugh left him. "Not going to happen." He bent his head and kissed her deeply, thoroughly, until she was writhing on the bed needing more. Reaching down, she wrapped her fingers around him and stroked, coaxing a deliciously male sound from his throat.

"You taste like a strawberry margarita," she murmured.

"I want to find out what you taste like," he said and slid down her body, kissing every inch of her as he went. Her jaw, her throat, her shoulder and collarbone. Her breasts. He spent long moments there, teasing, biting softly down on a nipple before drawing it into his mouth and sucking so that she arched off the bed.

"Mmm," he said, his voice low and hot. "You taste amazing." He nibbled a hip. Scraped his teeth over her belly, an inner thigh. Then the other.

And then in between.

She would've come right off the mattress if he hadn't had a hand on either of her hips holding her down, anchoring her to the bed as he had his merry way with her. Her entire body was tensed like a tightly coiled spring ready to snap and just when she thought she couldn't take any more, he slowed down and let her catch her breath.

Then he started over, again taking her to very edge and holding her there until she was rocking mindlessly, her hands fisted in his hair, shamelessly begging for him to finish her.

Which he did.

Twice.

When he finally crawled back up her body, he kissed her before rolling on a condom while she watched—which was shockingly, incredibly arousing all by itself—and when he was done, his gaze swept over her as he gave himself a long, slow stroke.

Sitting up, she nudged his hands away and took over. His head fell back as a rough groan escaped him. When she leaned forward and licked his nipple in tune to another stroke, he wrapped an arm low around her hips and lifted her, guiding himself home.

He sank in deep. So deep she cried out his name and clutched at him. "Okay?" he asked, holding himself utterly still, the strain of doing so in every line of his gorgeous, hard body. "Do you want to stop?"

"Stop and I'll kill you, right here in Mexico where I could probably even get away with it."

His laugh was rough, as was hers. The sound must have triggered something inside him because he laid her back on the mattress, leaned over her, and drove into her, thrusting long and hard and deep. She wrapped her legs around his waist and met him stroke for stroke, crying out as he took her to paradise.

SEAN MIGHT AS well have just been hit by a runaway Mack truck. He felt that gobsmacked by what had just happened between him and Lotti. It'd been . . . incredible. Like holy shit, off the rails, into the stratosphere incredible. He glanced over at her and found her eyes closed. She was breathing like she'd just run a mile. Her skin was flushed and she was damp with sweat, her hair rioting wildly around her face. She looked thoroughly fucked and thoroughly sated.

And she'd never looked more beautiful. "Lotti."

She opened her eyes. They were dazed and glossy and unfocused. "Hmm?"

He rose up on an elbow and leaned over her. "Tell me that was real. That you didn't . . ."

Her eyes narrowed. "Didn't what?"

"Fake it."

She blinked and then . . . laughed. She laughed so hard that she started to choke and he had to yank her upright and get her some water, which she proceeded to *also* choke on.

It was an excruciating five minutes later before she could talk and he was waiting with a barely tethered impatience.

"You think I faked it?" she asked incredulously. "Twice?"

"Three times," he said.

She blushed a little, but overall looked so pleased with herself that he relaxed.

"Okay then," he said. "So you didn't."

"Wait a minute," she said. "What if I had? What then?"

"We'd start over from the beginning."

She stared at him and then gave a slow, sexy smile, and he felt his heart roll over and expose its underbelly.

"Then I definitely faked them," she said and lay back. "So you'd better start over from the beginning."

LYING THERE WITH Sean after round two, waiting for their heart rates to recover from stroke level, Lotti kept expecting him to get up and leave.

But he didn't.

Instead, he straightened the covers that they'd destroyed and then climbed back in bed with her.

"What are you doing?" she asked as he pulled her in close.

"Worried?" he asked.

When was he going to learn—she was *always* worried. Although a good amount of that worry faded, replaced by something else as he nuzzled at her jaw, making a very male, very sexy satisfied sound deep in his throat. "Are you . . . cuddling me?" she asked.

"Trying," he said, sounding amused.

She allowed it because who the hell was she kidding, she loved the way he was holding her, loved the feel of his warm, strong body cradling hers. But she did feel that she needed to remind them both of something. "You know that what happens in Mexico stays in Mexico, right?"

"Sure," he said.

She opened her mouth to say "no *really,*" but he stroked her hair from her face and smiled at her. "Not a cuddler, huh?"

"I like affection," she admitted. *Way too much.* "But you should know, I'm kind of . . . well, emotionally unavailable."

"Is that right?"

"Yes."

"And what does that mean exactly, 'kind of emotionally unavailable'?" he asked, looking sincerely interested, so she gave him the truth.

"It means I like it when you hold me," she said. "But I don't really want to answer any questions. Or talk," she added, wanting to cover all her bases.

He grinned and kissed her. "Maybe I'll wear you down."

Her biggest fear was that he already had. "Don't count on it."

"Okay, tough girl," he said softly, nuzzling at her throat. "No questions. No talking. You go ahead and give ignoring what's still between us your best shot. I'll wait right here."

MUCH LATER LOTTI came awake suddenly. The last thing she remembered was . . . well, riding Sean like a wild bronco. But she was alone in her bed.

So he'd left after all.

Okay, she got it. She really did. But wait a minute. There was a dim light coming from the direction of her kitchen table.

Sean sat at it, working on his tablet. "Sorry," he said. "Did I wake you?"

"No." Realizing she was bare ass naked, she grabbed the sheet and pulled it to her chin.

This made him smile. He was sitting on one of her chairs, which he'd turned around so his chest was leaning into the back of it, wearing nothing but those sexy as hell board shorts.

"What are you doing?" she asked.

"I just got ordained online."

She blinked.

"To marry Finn and Pru," he said. "Now I'm writing the ceremony. Or trying." He ran a hand down his face, making her take a closer look at him.

He looked . . . exhausted. And tense with stress.

She carefully slid out of the bed, keeping the sheet wrapped around her as she did. Moving to stand behind him, she leaned over his shoulder to look at his screen, but he cleared it.

"You're embarrassed," she said in surprise.

He grimaced. "Let's just say talking about love and commitment is new for me. Very new." Reaching back, he hooked an arm around her hips to keep her close.

"You're having regrets," she murmured, and utterly unable to help herself, slid her hands to his broad, bare shoulders.

He moaned and leaned into her fingers as they dug into his tense muscles. "Regrets, yes. Lots of them, actually," he said.

This had her freezing. She went to remove her hands from him, but he reached up and entwined their fingers, giving a little tug so that she leaned over him. Turning his head, he looked into her eyes as he lifted her hand to his mouth and brushed his lips across her palm. "Not about last night, Lotti. I have no regrets there. Not a single one."

She let out a breath she hadn't realized she'd been holding. She didn't have regrets either. What had happened between them had been . . . amazing. And it'd also told her something she'd already known about herself but hadn't accepted.

Regardless of how much time had gone by, regardless of her cocky talk of being emotionally unavailable, she was still greatly, deeply emotionally invested in Sean O'Riley. "If it's not me, what are you regretting?" she asked.

He gently squeezed her fingers. "How I handled things with you all those years ago. What a shithead I was in general." He pushed his tablet away. "That I can't pay my brother back for all he's done for me."

She shouldn't have felt surprised. Even after what had happened between her and Sean that long-ago night, she'd still known he was a good guy. But now, seeing the man he'd turned into, how he'd shed the anger and resentment and his adolescence and had gotten himself a life, a good one, warmed her. "It sounds to me as if you've been doing just that," she said, "paying him back, and have been for a few years now. You work with him running the pub. In fact, it sounds like you take care of him every bit as much as he ever took care of you."

He started to shake his head, and she leaned in and gave him a soft kiss. "Sean, I'm watching you work your ass off to give him the wedding he deserves. You're doing everything in your power to give it to him because you love him. It's . . ."

"What?"

"Moving," she said.

He turned around to face her and pulled her into his lap, running a hand through her hair, tucking it all back behind her ear. His knuckles slid along the outer shell and she suppressed a shiver of desire that slid slowly down her spine.

Brushing a soft kiss against her temple, he wrapped his arms around her and pressed his face into her throat. "I thought coming to Napa was such a mistake," he said. "I wanted to take everyone to Vegas for the weekend. Looking back, I can't believe how close I came to never running into you again."

She was quiet a moment, thinking about that. "I'm glad you came here," she finally admitted.

He squeezed her tight. "Me too."

They sat there together quietly, and she relaxed into him. "Show me?" she murmured, gesturing to the tablet.

He hesitated and then brought his screen up.

She stared at it in confusion. "It's . . ."

"Blank?" he asked. "Yeah." He huffed out a sigh. "I keep deleting everything I come up with."

"Why?"

"Because when it comes right down to it, I don't know shit about everlasting love."

"I've seen you with your friends, Sean. I've seen you with Finn. You're a very tight-knit group and you seem to be an important part of it. They all love you, especially your brother."

He didn't say anything to this but he did meet her gaze, his own revealing a vulnerability that reminded her of the younger Sean. "Tell me some of the things you've written and deleted," she said.

He looked away from her, facing the blank screen. "They're two of the strongest people I've ever met. They had to be. They each suffered some pretty big losses early on, which left them no choice but to pick themselves up and carry on." He paused. "That they found each other is a miracle. Neither of them were exactly open to the idea of love." He paused again and still she didn't speak, not wanting to interrupt him, but also unbearably moved.

"It wasn't love at first sight," Sean said quietly. "But I think that's the point. First, they had to learn to like each other. And then trust each other." His voice was a little thick. Gruff. "Love born of that, trust, is an everlasting kind of love."

Lotti's throat was tight with emotion. She still didn't speak because now she literally couldn't.

Sean sighed and nuzzled his jaw to hers. "You can see why I'm having trouble."

"No." Cupping his face, she lifted it and looked into his eyes, letting him see the emotion in hers. "It's incredible, Sean. You're incredible."

He closed his eyes and shook his head so she whispered it again against his stubble-roughened jaw. And then yet again against his mouth.

His arms came around her hard. "Careful," he murmured huskily, eyes still closed. "Our positions are reversed this time. After last night and this morning—and though the sex was amazing, that's not what I'm referring to—*you're* going to leave *me* with the broken heart." He opened his eyes and unerringly leveled her with his stark gaze.

She stared at him right back. "Don't tease me," she whispered.

"I'm not teasing."

And indeed, there was no light of joviality in his expression, not a drop, and she swallowed hard. "I didn't sleep with you to get back at you, Sean."

"No, you slept with me because you wanted a one-night stand with a surfer." A ghost of a smile crossed his lips. "Mission accomplished."

"Okay, so we know why I slept with you," she said. "But why did you sleep with me?"

He held her gaze. "Maybe I thought you might fall for me again and I'd get it right this time."

Her heart squeezed. "Sean—"

He put a finger to her lips. "Don't burst my bubble yet," he said and slowly fisted his hands in her hair, carefully pulling her in so that they shared their next breath of air. "Not until I'm finished giving you everything I've got."

"How much more could you possibly have?" she asked, shifting in his lap, humming in pleasure at what she found. "Wait. You don't need to tell me, I think I've just found out for myself."

With a snort, he rose from the chair in one easy movement, her still in his arms. He turned to the bed and tossed her onto it, retaining his grip on the sheet wrapped around her.

This meant she landed butt naked in the middle of the mattress. She bounced and let out a squeak, trying to roll over and grab the covers.

But Sean was quicker, snatching the blanket, dropping it on the floor behind him, along with the sheet.

His smile was badass wicked and filled with trouble as he put a knee on the bed and began to crawl toward her with nefarious intent in his sharp gaze.

With another squeak, she started to scramble to the edge of the bed but then stopped. What was she doing? She *wanted* him to catch her. So she waited until he was close and then *she* pounced on *him*, pushing him down to the bed and claiming the victor's spot.

His hands at her hips, he smiled up at her. "You think you've got me?"

She took his hands in hers and flattened them above his head, stretching herself along the length of him. Still holding him down, her gaze locked on his, she lifted up and took him inside her body. "I know I do."

"Oh fuck, Lotti." He arched up into her, his neck corded, his face a mask of intense pleasure. "You do, you've got me. Do with me whatever you want."

So she did.

Chapter Eight

A FEW HOURS LATER, Sean stood in the large living room of the B&B, taking in the room with a narrowed eye. Christmas on crack, check. Candles everywhere, check. Chairs pulled from every room in the house arranged with an aisle for Pru to walk toward Finn, check. Music softly playing from a wireless speaker that was Bluetoothed to his phone, check.

There was no electricity, but they didn't need it. Outside, rain drummed steadily against the old Victorian, adding to the ambiance.

"What do you think?" Lotti asked at his side, sounding nervous.

He turned to her and shook his head with a low laugh. "I think it's perfect."

Her smile was warm and relieved, and the vise that had been around his heart since this morning when he'd realized the craziest thing—that he was falling for her all over again—tightened.

The roads were being cleared even as they stood here. Estimated time of opening was tomorrow morning. This meant that at best he had twenty-four hours to make her start to fall too.

"It all looks good," she said. "You pulled it off."

"*We* pulled it off."

She turned to him, her smile fading, but before she could speak, Finn came up the makeshift aisle. He was in dress pants and a slate gray button down—the same that he'd worn to the bachelor/bachelorette party. Looking uncharacteristically nervous, he fussed with his tie until it was crooked.

"Here," Sean said and knocked his brother's hands away. "I've got it. What the hell's wrong with you?" he asked when he realized Finn was sweating. "You wanted this."

"Still do," Finn said. "More than I want anything else in the entire world." His serious gaze met Sean's. "This is the most important thing I'll ever do."

And *that* was why he was nervous, Sean realized. "Hey man, you got this. And I've got you. So no worries."

Finn let out a long, shaky exhale and nodded. "Thanks."

Sean turned to Lotti and found her studying him with a look he'd never seen before, like maybe she was proud of him. He had to admit, he didn't hate that.

"And shouldn't you be the anxious one?" Finn asked

Sean. "You're the guy who has to marry us. All I've gotta do is say 'I do.'"

"True," Sean said.

"I mean it's you who has to make sure it all happens here today," Finn went on. "That nothing goes wrong, that it's absolutely perfect. So . . . are you? Nervous?"

Well he was now. "How hard can it be?" he asked with what he hoped was a calm voice. No need to share with the class that he was shaking in his boots. "Take this ring, I thee wed, cherish and obey, yadda yadda, right?" he asked.

Finn laughed. "Dude, if you put 'obey' in the vows, Pru's going to kill you where you stand."

"Oh, I had it for *your* part of the vows, not hers."

Finn grabbed him in a headlock and they tussled for a minute, like old times.

And then, less than a half an hour later, Archer was walking Pru down the aisle toward Finn. Seeing the love shining so brilliantly between the two of them after saying "with the power invested in me by Get-Ordained.com, Finn, kiss your bride!" Watching as they laughed and Pru jumped into Finn's arms while everyone hugged. Sean knew he'd never forget a minute of this trip.

Lotti came up to his side and he looked at her. Huh. She *was* proud of him. "You were amazing," she said.

He didn't quite feel amazing. He felt . . . something he couldn't quite define. Not that there was time to think because they all moved back the furniture, kicked up the music, danced, drank, and ate.

And then danced, drank, and ate some more.

Watching, feeling oddly enough a little bit like he was on the outside looking in, Sean realized what was wrong.

He was *lonely*, even while surrounded by the people who meant the most to him in the world. How that could be the case, he honestly had no idea. He picked up the bottle of Corona in front of him and took a long pull. It'd been years since he'd been intoxicated, but tonight was definitely the end of a long dry spell. He smiled as Finn and Pru made their way around the makeshift dance floor. He'd never seen Finn so happy.

Never.

They made a great couple, appreciating and recognizing what they had, what they'd worked so hard for. It was their night and no one deserved it more.

Sean's eyes searched out Lotti for the thousandth time. She wore a midnight colored dress, short and molded perfectly to her soft curves and showing off some gorgeous legs that he wanted wrapped around him. She'd started out the evening with her hair carefully twisted at the back of her head. Some of it had escaped. Tendrils framed her flushed face and fell over her bare shoulders and back, teasing her skin.

She was so beautiful she made his chest hurt. But ever since the ceremony, during which she had adorably teared up, she'd been different. Holding herself back.

The rancher from next door had showed up a few minutes ago with another case of beer that he'd found in his back refrigerator. Lotti was talking to him, thanking him, a soft smile playing at the corners of her mouth.

It didn't matter how many times Sean saw her smile, he still felt the pleasure from it like it was the first time, back at that football game . . . He'd had no right to touch her that night, but he had.

He had even less right to touch her now. He'd had his chance and he'd walked away from her.

Man, he'd been such a stupid sixteen-year-old punk.

But God, he hoped like hell that second chances were really a thing as he finished off his beer and made his way over to her. This wasn't going to be on the top ten list of the smartest things he'd ever done, but at that moment he didn't care.

Archer stepped into his path. "Whatcha doing?"

"Nothing," Sean said.

"Nothing, or you're about to go interrupt a really great woman from getting a dance invite?"

Sean met Archer's gaze and Archer went brows up. "We're leaving here soon enough," Archer said.

Like Sean didn't know. "And?"

"And . . . don't needlessly complicate things for her."

Sean looked over at Lotti, who was smiling up into the rancher's face. "Archer?"

"Yeah?"

"Remember when you *needlessly* complicated Elle's life?"

Archer sighed.

"Just tell me this—what would you have done if I'd tried to stop you?" Sean asked.

Archer conceded gracefully. "Probably taken out a few of your front teeth." He backed up a step, hands in the air, signaling that Sean should carry on as he planned.

So Sean once again headed toward Lotti. He'd made his life about freedom and no complications. But he'd been fighting a restlessness, an aching loneliness for a while now. He hadn't known what to do about it, but he knew now.

He walked up to Lotti and the rancher just in time to hear the guy ask her to dance. "Can I cut in?" Sean asked, not that he was going to take no for an answer.

The rancher's gaze slid first to Lotti, who was still just staring up at Sean, before nodding curtly and stepping away from her.

Sean took Lotti's hand and brought her to the dance floor. Her eyes were guarded and she felt a little stiff in his arms as he pulled her in close for the slow song.

"You had all night to ask me to dance," she said. "Why did you pick that very moment?"

"Why are you already distancing yourself from me?" he asked instead of responding to the question for which he didn't have any good answer to give. "I haven't even left yet."

"But you're going to," she said.

Yeah. She had him there. He pulled her in close, drinking in her familiar scent, molding his body to hers so that he felt the exact second she melted into him. When she sighed, he knew he wasn't alone in this, no matter what she wanted him to believe. They had something, something deep and meaningful and everlasting. Running a hand down the length of her back, he closed his eyes to savor the feel of her bare skin beneath his fingers.

"Sean?"

He opened his eyes and realized every gaze in the room was on them. He slid them all a hard look that said *mind your own fucking business for once* and led Lotti over to a more secluded part of the room, on the other side of the huge Christmas tree, where he could continue to hold on to her without their avid audience.

"So about the distance thing," he said.

"We're not going there," she said. "You're leaving. The end."

He looked into her eyes. "Are you saying you have no interest in letting me be a part of your life?"

"But see, that's just it. You're *not* a part of my life," she said. "You're a fantasy. One that's about to go poof and vanish."

"It doesn't have to be like that, Lotti."

She gave him a get real look. "Yeah. I've heard that before."

Okay, he deserved her disbelief and probably a lot more. But he knew this wasn't about him, or even her feelings for him. "You've got cold feet again," he said. "And no one would blame you for that, Lotti. No one. But—"

"I've always rushed too fast," she said. "Rushed to my happily ever after, and it's never worked out for me."

"It only takes one," he said.

She stared at him like he'd lost his mind. "Stop doing this."

"Stop doing what? Wanting you? Wanting you to want me?"

"It was just a weekend."

He looked into her eyes and saw old hurts and new fears. Fears that he might hurt her . . . again. Legitimate. He leaned in and touched his mouth to the shell of her ear. "It feels like a lot more than a weekend," he confessed.

She didn't say anything to this but she did settle in against him eventually relaxing in his arms. After that he let the beat of the music carry them. He felt ridiculous when he started to dread the end of the song. He didn't want to lose the physical contact, and as if maybe she felt the same, her hands tightened around his neck and she pressed her face into his throat.

"I'm sorry, Lotti," he said. "So damned sorry for what I did to you."

"No, I was messed up, thinking that my first lover was The One. No sixteen-year-old boy could've lived up to my expectations. Hell, even now, no one could. In fact . . ." She shook her head. "I make sure they can't. My fiancé . . ."

"I know," he said. "He was an ass too. Leaving you a week before your wedding—"

"It was my fault, Sean."

"No. No way."

"Yes way," she said. She grimaced and shook her head. "I kept changing the date of the wedding, pushing it back. It was my way of sabotaging. It's what I do, I push people away. And I'm good at it, Sean." She stepped back, and he could see in her eyes it was more than the song ending.

They were ending before they'd even gotten started. "Wait," he said. "What happened to eating the cookies, to reading books for pleasure, to singing in the rain and jumping into the puddles?" He paused until she met his gaze. "What happened to falling in love with a blast from your past?"

"I . . . I never said that last part. Sean—"

He could see in her eyes what she was about to say. "Lotti, don't—"

"I promised myself I'd start learning from the mistakes of my past instead of repeating them." And then she stepped out of his arms and walked away.

Just as he'd once done to her.

THE NEXT MORNING dawned gray and dark, but nothing was falling out of the sky at least. Sean reached for his phone and checked the weather and roads.

The worst of the storm had passed. The roads were a mess, many still impassable but they were starting to slowly let people through. They could get out.

And sure enough, an hour later, Sean stood watching as his friends loaded up the van. He had his bag packed, but he wasn't ready to leave.

He wasn't ever going to be ready to leave.

Determined to tell Lotti that very thing, he turned to go find her—but she was right there, a nervous smile curving her mouth. "Can I talk to you for a sec?" she asked.

"You can talk to me for as long as you want." *Forever,* he thought. *Talk to me forever so I don't have to leave.*

She swallowed hard and looked down at her clipboard. "Well, I've been thinking."

"Which explains the smoke coming out of your ears."

She let out a low laugh. "Yeah. I do tend to overthink things. I like to obsess over every decision until it's nearly impossible to make. Which is why I'm changing things up." She met his gaze. "I overthought this weekend."

Unable to help himself, he closed the distance between them and cupped her jaw. "There's nothing to overthink. What we shared here was a second chance, and I don't intend to let it pass us by." He leaned in and kissed her. "I want to see you again, Lotti. As soon as you'll let me. I'm going to call. Text. Email. FaceTime. Whatever it takes to show you I'm serious. We're only forty minutes away from each other. That's nothing. *Nothing,*" he repeated, setting a finger over her lips when she opened her mouth. "And I know you have no reason at all to believe me, to believe *in* me, but it's okay. All I need is some time to show you."

She took a gentle nip out of his finger. "I want to see you again too."

His heart leapt. "Yeah?"

"Yeah and . . . well, I sort of I have a confession." She pulled a piece of paper from her clipboard. Her Cabo itinerary. "I thought we could rebook my flights," she said. "And add a plus one because I was hoping you'd come with. I mean, I know your brother just got married so you're undoubtedly in charge of the pub when you get back, so we can time it so that it works out for everyone. If you're interested . . ."

He had to pause because the emotion and relief and hope that flooded him took away his ability to speak for a second.

"I mean, I know it's a big deal to go on vacay together when we hardly know each other, but it doesn't have to be any sort of pressure or anything," she said softly, letting him see the emotion and hope in her eyes. But there were nerves too. She was worried he'd say no.

"Yes," he said.

"Yes, you're okay with no pressure or yes to—"

"Yes to all of it," he said. "Everything. Whatever you want." And then he sealed the vow with a kiss.

Epilogue

CABO WAS EVERYTHING Napa hadn't been. Warm, sunny . . . *perfect*, Lotti thought on a dreamy sigh. Sean had upgraded their accommodations to a villa with a private pool and its own access to the beach. He said he'd done it because he wanted to go skinny-dipping with her, but she knew there was another reason as well.

He didn't want anything to remind her of the honeymoon this trip had been planned for, showing another surprising side to Sean O'Riley. A sweet side.

There were other ways in which he'd made sure that this trip didn't remind her of anything in her past. Of course, most of those ways had occurred in bed. And on the kitchenette counter. And the patio lounger. And the shower . . .

At the moment, she was on the lounger sunning while Sean was on the phone, checking in at home. She flopped over on her stomach and untied the back of her bikini so she wouldn't get a tan line. The air was warm and salty and she could hear the waves, which lulled her into dozing off.

She woke up as two big, slightly callused hands ran up and down her body and smiled. "Mmm, Thor," she murmured. "Don't stop."

A low, masculine growl had her smiling. "Don't worry," she murmured. "My boyfriend's on the phone. We've got plenty of time."

She squeaked when she was lifted in the air and tossed over Sean's shoulder like a sack of potatoes and carried toward the pool.

"Oh no," she said, laughing. "I can't get my hair wet before we go out to dinner."

He didn't slow down.

"Sean! I'm not kidding! You're closing in on batshit crazy if you think I've time to fix this mop before those fancy reservations you made—"

He was still moving and all she could see was the smooth, sinewy expanse of his tanned back and those low-riding board shorts emphasizing his great ass. "Stop!" She was laughing so hard she could scarcely talk. "Sean, wait! I take it back! You're not closing in on batshit crazy . . ."

He paused in his progress and slid a hand to her ass. "No?"

"No," she said. "I'd never imply that you'd do anything halfway." She paused. "You're *completely* batshit crazy."

His shoulders were shaking with laughter as he put her down on the top step inside the pool. The water was a perfect seventy-eight degrees so she felt no twinge of guilt when she smiled up at him sweetly, sexily, making a promise with her eyes, causing him to smile at her in return as she . . .

Shoved him backward into the pool.

It would've been the perfect move if he hadn't been as fast as a cat, a big, bad mountain cat who snagged her around the ankle and took her in with him.

She laughed at the shock of the water and was still laughing when he kissed her. It was one of those kisses that started off sweet but then escalated quickly. Her bikini top was floating away on the water before she could blink and Sean slid his tongue over a taut nipple, making goose bumps race along her skin.

"Give me a chance," he said against her lips.

She pulled back to meet his gaze, having to blink a couple of times before the words he'd spoken could sink in. "What?"

He cupped her face in the palm of his hand. His thumb stroked over her cheekbone as he studied her eyes. "I want you to give me a chance."

"A chance at what?"

Shifting so that he could press his forehead to hers, he said one word. "You."

Her breath caught. "Sean," she breathed.

"Because you've got me," he said. "All of me. I'm falling in love you, Lotti, heart and soul. I know it's too soon for you. I know you're scared. I know you're not sure about me. I know it's going to take time, but I've got that to give and more. I can wait. You're worth it."

She couldn't tear her gaze off him, this incredible, amazing man who'd had her heart from all those years ago. "We must both be crazy."

"Because . . . ?"

"Because I'm falling for you too, Sean." There were other words that needed to be said. A lot. They'd have to talk more, but she had that one thing of his that she had begun to crave. His heart. And for now that was enough.

**Keep reading for a sneak peek at the
next Heartbreaker Bay romance**

ABOUT THAT KISS

When love drives you crazy . . .

When sexy Joe Malone never calls after their explosive kiss, Kylie shoves him out of her mind. Until she needs a favor, and it's a doozy. Something precious to her has been stolen and there's only one person with the unique finder-and-fixer skills that can help—Joe. It means swallowing her pride and somehow trying to avoid the temptation to throttle him—or seduce him.

the best thing to do . . .

No, Joe didn't call after the kiss. He's the fun time guy, not the forever guy. And Kylie, after all she's been through, deserves a good man who will stay. But everything about Kylie makes it damned hard to focus, and though his brain knows what he has to do, his heart isn't getting the memo.

is enjoy the ride

As Kylie and Joe go on the scavenger hunt of their lives, they discover surprising things about each other. Now, the best way for them to get over "that kiss" might just be to replace it with a hundred more.

Chapter 1

#LifeIsLikeABoxOfChocolates

KYLIE MASTERS WATCHED him walk into her shop like he owned it while simultaneously pretending not to notice him. A tricky balancing act that she'd gotten good at. Problem was, like it or not, her attention was caught and captured by the six-foot, leanly muscled, scowling guy now standing directly in front of her, hands shoved in his pockets, body language clearly set to Frustrated Male.

She sighed, gave up the ridiculous pretense of being engrossed by her phone, and met his gaze. She was supposed to smile and ask how she could help him. That's what they all did when it was their turn to work the front counter at Reclaimed Woods. They were to show potential clients their custom-made goods when what they really wanted was to be in the back workshop on their own, individual projects. Kylie's specialty was dining room sets, which meant she wore a thick apron and goggles to protect herself and was perpetually covered in sawdust.

And she did mean *covered* in sawdust. Wood flakes dusted her hair, stuck to her exposed arms, and if she'd been wearing any makeup today, they'd have been stuck to her face as well. In short, she was not looking how she wanted to be looking while facing this man again. Not even close. "Joe," she said in careful greeting.

He gave her a single head nod.

Okay, so he wasn't going to talk first. Fine. She'd be the grownup today. "What can I do for you?" she asked, fairly certain he wasn't here to shop for furniture. He wasn't exactly the domesticated type.

Joe ran a hand through his hair so that the military short, dark silky strands stood straight up. He wore a black t-shirt stretched over broad shoulders, loose over tight abs, untucked over cargos that emphasized his mile-long legs. He was built like the soldier he'd been not too long ago, as if keeping fit was his job—which given what he did for a living, it absolutely was. He shoved his mirrored sunglasses to the top of his head, revealing ice blue eyes that could be hard as stone when working but she knew that they could also soften when he was amused, aroused, or having fun. He was none of those three things at the moment.

"I need a birthday present for Molly," he said.

Molly was his sister, and from what Kylie knew of

the Malone family, they were close. Everyone knew this and adored the both of them. Kylie herself adored Molly.

She did *not* adore Joe.

"Okay," she said. "What do you want to go for her?"

"She made me a list." Joe pulled the list written in Molly's neat scrawl from one of his many cargo pants pockets.

Bday wishlist:

—Puppies. (Yes, plural!)
—Shoes. I *lurve* shoes. Must be as hot as Elle's.
—$$$.
—Concert tickets to Beyoncé.
—A release from the crushing inevitability of death.
—The gorgeous wooden inlay mirror made by Kylie.

"It's not her birthday for several weeks," Joe said as Kylie read the list. "But she said the mirror's hanging behind the counter and I didn't want it to be sold before I could buy it." His sharp blue eyes searched the wall behind her. "That one," he said, pointing to an intricately wood lined mirror that Kylie had indeed made. "She says she fell in love with it. Not all that surprising since your work's amazing."

Kylie did her best to keep this from making her glow with pleasure. She and Joe had known each other casually for the year that they'd both been working in this building. Until two nights ago, they'd never done anything but annoy each other. So that he thought of her as amazing was news to her. "I didn't know you were even aware of my work."

Instead of answering, his gaze narrowed in on the price tag hanging off the mirror and he let out a low whistle.

"I don't get to set the prices here," she said, irritating herself with her defensive tone. She had no idea why she let him drive her so crazy with little to no effort on his part, but she did her best to not examine the reasons for this.

Ever.

Joe had been special ops and still had most of his skills, skills he used on his job at an investigation and securities firm upstairs, where he was, for the lack of a better term, a professional finder and fixer. He was a calm and impenetrable badass on the job, and a calm, impenetrable smartass off of it. On the worst of days, he made her feel like a seesaw. On the best of days, he made her feel things she liked to shove deep, *deep* down, because going there with him would be like jumping out of a plane—thrilling, exciting . . . and then certain dismemberment and death.

While she was thinking about this and other things she shouldn't be thinking, Joe was eyeballing the opened box of chocolates on the counter, which a client had brought in earlier. A little card said: *Help Yourself!* and his gaze locked in on the last Bordeaux—her favorite. She'd been saving it as a reward if she made it all day without wanting to strangle anyone.

Mission failed. "It'll go right to your hips," she warned.

He met her gaze, his own amused. "You worried about my body, Kylie?"

She used the excuse to look him over. Not exactly a hardship. He was lean, solid muscle. Rumors were that he'd done some MMA fighting right after his service and she believed it. He was perfect and they both knew it. "I didn't want to mention it," she said, "but I think you're starting to get a spare tire."

"Is that right?" He cocked his head, eyes amused. "A spare tire, huh? Anything else?"

"Wellllllll . . . maybe a little junk in the trunk."

He out and out grinned at that, the cocky bastard. "Then maybe we should *share* the chocolate," he said and offered the Bordeaux to her, bringing it up to her lips.

Against her better judgment, she took a bite, resisting the urge to also sink her teeth into his fingers.

With a soft laugh that told her he'd read her mind, he popped the other half into his own mouth and then licked some melted chocolate off his thumb with a suctioning sound that went straight to her nipples, which was *super* annoying.

"So," he said when he'd swallowed. "The mirror. I'll take it." Reaching into yet another mystery pockets, he pulled out a credit card. "Wrap it up."

"You can't have it."

At this, he studied her for a surprised beat, like maybe he'd never been told no before in his life.

And hell, looking like he did, he probably hadn't been.

"Okay," he said. "I get it. It's because I never called, right?"

She pushed his hand—and the credit card in it—away. But not before she felt the heat and the easy strength of him, both of which only further annoyed her. "Wrong," she said. "Not everything's about you, Joe."

"True. This is clearly about *us*," he said. "And that kiss."

Oh hell no. He didn't just bring it up like that, like it was some throw away event. She pointed to the door. "Get out."

He just smiled. And didn't get out.

Damn it. She'd grounded herself from thinking about that kiss. That one, drunken, very stupid kiss that haunted her dreams and way too many awake moments as well. But it all flooded back to her now, releasing a bunch of stupid endorphins and everything. She inhaled a deep breath, locked her knees *and* her heart, and mentally tossed away the key. "What kiss?"

He gave her a get real look.

"Oh, *that* kiss." She shrugged as nonchalantly as she reached for her water bottle. "I barely remember it."

"Funny," he said in a voice of pure sin. "Cuz it rocked my world."

She choked on her water, coughing and sputtering.

"The mirror's still not for sale," she finally managed to wheeze out, wiping her mouth.

She'd rocked his world?

His warm, amused gaze met hers, going smoky and dangerously charismatic. "I could change your mind."

"On the mirror or the kiss?" she asked before she could stop herself.

"Either. Both."

She had no doubt. "The mirror's already sold," she said. "The new owner's coming for it today."

The buyer just happened to be Spence Baldwin, who owned the building in which they stood. The Pacific Pier Building to be exact, one of the oldest in the Cow Hollow District of San Francisco. Since the building housed an eclectic mix of businesses on the first and second floors, residential apartments on the third and fourth floors, all built around a cobblestone courtyard with a fountain that had been there back in the days when there'd still been actual cows in Cow Hollow, the entire place went a lot like the song—everyone knew everyone's name.

In any case, Spence had bought the mirror for his girlfriend Colbie, not that Kylie was going to tell Joe that. For one thing, Spence and Joe were good friends and Spence might let Joe have the mirror.

And though she didn't know why, Kylie didn't want Joe to have it. Okay, so she did know why. Things came easy to Joe. Good looking, exciting job . . . hell, *life* came easy to him.

"I'll commission a new one," Joe said, still looking unconcerned. "You can make another just like it, right?"

Yes, and normally a commissioned piece would be a thrill. Kylie wasn't all that established yet and could certainly use the work. But instead of being excited, she felt . . . unsettled. Because if she agreed to the job, there'd be ongoing contact. Conversations.

And here was the thing—she didn't trust him. No, that wasn't right. She didn't trust *herself* with him. *She'd rocked his world?* Because he'd sent hers spinning and the truth was, it'd take no effort at all to once again end up glued to him at the lips. "I'm sorry, but maybe you can get Molly . . ." She eyed the list again. "Puppies."

And speaking of puppies, just then from the back room came a high-pitched bark. Vinnie was up from his nap. Next came the pitter patter of paws scrambling. At the doorway between the shop and the showroom, he skidded to a stop and lifted a paw, poking at the empty air in front of his face.

Not too long ago, her undersized rescue pup had run face first into a glass door. So now he went through this pantomime routine in every doorway he came to. And she did mean every doorway. Poor Vinnie had PTSD, and she was his emotional support human.

When Vinnie was thoroughly satisfied that there was no hidden glass to run into, he was off and galloping again, a dark brown blur skidding around the corner of the counter like a cat on linoleum. Half French Bulldog and half Muppet, no one had ever told him that he was under a foot tall and twelve pounds soaking wet. He actually thought he was the big man on campus, and he smiled the whole way as he ran straight for Kylie, tongue lolling out the side of his mouth, drool dribbling in his wake.

Heart melting, Kylie started to bend to reach for him, but he flew right by her.

Joe had squatted low, hands held out for the dog, who never so much glanced over at Kylie as he took a flying leap into Joe's waiting arms. Arms that she knew were warm and strong and gave great hugs, dammit.

Man and pup straightened, rubbing faces together for a moment while Kylie did her best not to melt. Like most French Bulldog's, Vinnie's expression often read glum. She called it his RBF—resting bitch face. But he was actually the opposite of glum, and the mischievous, comical, amiable light in his eyes revealed that.

"Hey little man," Joe murmured, flashing that killer smile of his at her pup, who was valiantly attempting to lick his face off. Joe laughed and the sound caused an answering tug from deep inside Kylie, which was maddening.

She had no idea what was up with her hormones lately, but luckily they weren't in charge, her brain was. And her brain wasn't interested in Joe, excellent kisser or not. See, she had a long history with his kind, that being fast, wild, fun and . . . *dangerous.* Not her own personal history, but her mother's, and she refused to be the apple who fell too close to the tree.

"I'll pay extra," Joe said, still loving up on Vinnie to the dog's utter delight. "To commission a new mirror."

"It doesn't work like that," she said. "I've got jobs in front of you, jobs I have to finish on a schedule. A mirror I haven't yet even started isn't for sale."

"Everything's for sale," Joe said.

And how well she knew it. Shaking her head, she reached beneath the front counter and pulled a miniature tennis ball from her bag, waving it in front of Vinnie, who began to try to swim through the air to get to the ball.

"Cheater," Joe chastened mildly, but obligingly set Vinnie down. The dog immediately snorted in excitement and raced to Kylie, quickly going through his entire repertoire of tricks without pause, sitting, offering a paw to shake, lying down, rolling over . . .

"Cute," Joe said. "Does he fetch?"

"Of course." But truthfully, fetch wasn't Vinnie's strong suit. Grunting, farting, or snoring, *these* were his strong suits. He also often went spastic with no warning, zooming around a room in a frantic sprint until he started panting and then passed out. But he did not fetch, not that she'd admit it. "Vinnie, fetch," she said hopefully and tossed the ball a few feet away.

The dog gave a bark of sheer joy and gamefully took off, his short, bow legs churning up the distance. But as always, stopping was a problem and he overshot the ball. Overcorrecting to make the sharp turn, he careened right into a wall. He made a strong recovery though and went back for the ball.

Not that he returned it to Kylie. Nope. With the mini-tennis ball barely fitting in his mouth, Vinnie padded quickly into the back, presumably bringing his new treasure to his crate.

"Yeah, he's great at fetch," Joe said with a straight face.

"We're still working on it," she said just as a man came out from the back, joining them at the counter.

Gib was her boss, her friend, and her very long-time crush—though he only knew about the first two since dating her boss had never seemed like a smart idea—not that he'd ever asked her out or anything. He owned Reclaimed Woods and Kylie owed a lot to him. He'd hired her on here when she'd decided to follow her grandpa's footsteps and become a woodworker, giving her a chance to make a name for herself. He was a good guy and everything she'd ever wanted in a man—kind, patient, sweet.

In other words, Joe's polar opposite.

"Problem?" Gib asked.

"Just trying to make a purchase," Joe said, nodding to the mirror.

Gib looked at Kylie. "Told you it was remarkable."

It was pretty rare for Gib to hand out a compliment, and she felt her chest warm with surprise and pleasure. "Thanks."

He nodded and squeezed her hand in his, momentarily rendering her incapacitated because . . . he was touching her. He *never* touched her. "But the mirror's not available," he said to Joe.

"Yeah," Joe said, although his gaze didn't leave Kylie's. "I'm getting that."

Suddenly there was an odd and unfamiliar beat of tension in the air, one Kylie wasn't equipped to translate. Due to her parents being teens when she was born, she'd been primarily raised by her grandpa. She'd learned unusual skills for a little girl, like how to operate a planer and joiner without losing any fingers, and how to place bets at the horse races. She'd also she'd grown up into a quiet introvert, an old soul. She didn't open up easily and as a result, not once in her entire life had two guys been interested in her at the same time. In fact, for long stretches of time, there'd been *zero* guys interested.

So to have that bone-melting kiss with Joe still messing with her head and now Gib suddenly showing interest after . . . well, *years*, she felt like a panicked teenager. A sweaty, panicked teenager. She jabbed a finger towards the back. "I've, um . . . gotta get to work," she said and bailed like she was twelve years old instead of twenty-eight.

*Thank you for reading the Heartbreaker Bay series,
I hope you enjoy this bonus scene with Pru and Finn.
To understand this little tease, you should probably
read at least* Sweet Little Lies *first.*
—Jill ☺

PRU STARED DOWN at the diamond ring on her finger. It'd been there for a year, long enough that when she slid it off, like she did now, there was tan line on her finger. She ran the pad of her thumb over the whiter skin, thinking about her life before Finn and how it hadn't really been much of a life at all.

And then he'd come into it and turned her black and white world into full Technicolor and changed everything.

For the better.

So why then was she so out of sorts? She nearly jumped out of her own body when he spoke from behind her.

"Should I be worried?" he asked.

She hadn't heard him come home, hadn't heard him enter their bedroom. Anxious to see him, she turned to face him. And as it had from the very beginning, just the sight of the six-foot broad shouldered, dark eyed man drew her in and made her heart skip a beat. His eyes burned hot with an emotion she couldn't identify. She licked her suddenly dry lips and whispered "You're back."

"I am." Holding her gaze, Finn dropped his duffle bag to the floor of their place and stepped into her, putting his hands on her hips.

She ran hers up his chest and into his hair as she pressed her forehead to his, breathing him in, so happy to have him back. He and his brother Sean had taken a road trip and been gone two weeks.

It was an annual brother slash fishing thing, and she hadn't minded.

But what she *had* minded was the timing. She'd picked a fight just before he'd left, and then he'd been gone, lost to her at some isolated lake in Idaho where he'd had no reception.

No connection to her at all.

"I missed you," he said.

"Not as much as I missed you." She drew a deep breath and then held it, unsure of how to start. She was surprised when, without another word, he wrapped his arms around her tight and pressed his face into her throat, inhaling deeply, like he needed her more than his next breath.

It wasn't something he'd ever done before. No, that wasn't quite true. He'd taken comfort from her, yes, but . . . not like this, not where he actively sought it out.

"Pru," he whispered and lifted his head. He nuzzled into her, rubbing his scruffy jaw to hers, making a low, gruff sound that signified need and desire, and not just physical. When he finally kissed her, it was soft at first, inquisitive, letting her decide if she wanted this.

She'd never wanted anything more in her entire life, and she let him know by pressing closer, trying to wrap herself around him so she didn't ever have to let go. It wasn't until she pulled back to take off her sweater that he stopped her and met her gaze.

The honesty and lingering doubt in his eyes had Pru closing her eyes. "I wanted to tell you how sorry I was the minute you left," she said quietly, "but I'm so annoyingly stubborn. By the time I realized that I couldn't breathe again until I told you, you were already out of cell range."

He didn't say anything to this and her heart about stopped.

"I didn't mean it," she said. "What I said that day."

"You said that you didn't want to set a date for our wedding." His voice was quiet steel but she couldn't miss the hurt.

"I didn't mean it like that," she whispered.

"Then how did you mean it?"

"You know what the first thing people ask me when they see the ring on my finger? They want to know when we're getting married."

He gave her an almost smile. "I'd like to know the same."

"I didn't believe that." She let out a long, shaky breath. "That's why I picked the fight. I thought you wanted out."

He looked stunned. "Why would you think that? I asked you to marry me."

"Yes, but from that moment on, you never said anything more about what you wanted. You said it was up to me."

He opened his mouth to speak but she didn't give him the chance to. "Because Finn, I already insinuated myself into your life. I crowded you. I gave you no choice. I never picked a date because I didn't want to risk losing you by pushing you for more than you wanted to give. I said I'd marry you because I love you and I want to spend my life with you. If you want to stay engaged forever, that's good enough for me. The only thing I don't want is to lose you."

He stood there staring at her. When he didn't speak, she started to turn away but he caught her.

"Babe." His voice stopped her. "Wait."

She lifted her gaze to his and felt staggered by all she saw in his eyes. Frustration. Bemusement. Affection.

And love.

So much love it stole her breath.

"I thought about you the whole two weeks I was gone," he said, "every living minute, when I was freezing my ass off on that godforsaken lake at dawn trying to catch a fish for breakfast, when Sean wouldn't stop singing Rhianna and I wanted to strangle him, when I tried to fall asleep at night but could only think of you and wonder what you were doing, if you were changing your mind—"

"I wasn't." She shook her head, her eyes burning with tears. "I wouldn't."

"Good. Because sometimes I let myself remember what my world was like before you came into it and I don't want to go back to that. I need you in my life, Pru," he said, voice low and strained.

"I'm in. I'm all the way in," she breathed, tightening her grip on him. "I promise."

"You're my life, Pru. I need you with me, loving me. I didn't realize how much until I couldn't see you every day, touch you. With you, I'm less alone, and for the first time in my life I know what contentment feels like. You want me to set the date? Fine," he said fiercely. "I pick yesterday."

She choked out a laugh and he graced her with a smile that took her breath. She stepped into him and threw her arms around his neck, pulling his head down. "How about today instead?" she asked.

"That was my second choice," he said and covered her mouth with his.